"Why are you here?" Shay fought to keep her voice steady.

"Maybe I had the urge for dessert." Tyler grinned.

"Then you'll find more of a selection at SugarPie's."

"Could be. But maybe what I want's right here."

Once, she would have fallen for that line and hoped he wanted *her*. She was so over that now. So over him.

She slid open the freezer case and reached for an empty ice cream tub. It gave her an excuse to avoid his blue-eyed stare.

But Tyler stepped up beside her. "I'll get that."

"Thanks, but I'm pregnant, not incapacitated."

"I didn't think you were." He closed the freezer door. "Let's just say I'll scratch your back, you scratch mine."

He looked away, as if he'd only now realized what he had said. He cleared his throat a̶n̶ ̶ ̶ ̶ ̶ ̶ ̶ ̶ ̶ack at her. "I'll take care of this, th̶ ̶ ̶ ̶ ̶ ̶ ̶e of a few things for me."

Unfortunately, his̶ ̶ ̶ ̶ ̶ ̶ ̶ ̶ ̶ clearer only filled ̶ ̶ ̶ ̶ ̶ ̶ ̶ ̶ memories of their ̶ ̶ ̶ ̶ ̶ ̶

Suddenly, Shay didn̶ ̶ ̶ ̶ ̶ ̶ ̶ ̶ ̶o over Tyler Buckham.

Dear Reader,

If you've visited Cowboy Creek before, welcome back! And if this is your first time dropping in, have fun meeting Grandpa Jed and the rest of the gang at the Hitching Post Hotel.

As a writer, I love throwing my characters into the absolute worst situations for them. Take our heroine, Shay O'Neill, for example. She has sworn never to fall for a cowboy, and yet a smooth-talking wrangler steals her heart. For once in her life, she lets that heart rule her head. Then the playboy leaves town without a backward glance long before she discovers she's pregnant.

Rodeo rider Tyler Buckham is in for a few surprises of his own. As he has more reasons than most men for not wanting to settle down, he avoids permanent entanglements and always takes the proper precautions. But upon his return to Cowboy Creek, he learns the hard way that even the best-laid plans can fall to pieces...

I hope you enjoy Tyler's and Shay's attempts to put aside their differences to do what's best for their not one, not two, but three newborn babies.

You can find out more about the folks from the Hitching Post Hotel, as well as all my books, at: barbarawhitedaille.com. You can also reach me at my mailing address: PO Box 504, Gilbert, AZ 85299. I would love to hear from you!

All my best to you.

Until we meet again,

Barbara White Daille

THE COWBOY'S TRIPLE SURPRISE

———

BARBARA WHITE DAILLE

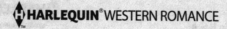

HARLEQUIN® WESTERN ROMANCE

Recycling programs
for this product may
not exist in your area.

ISBN-13: 978-0-373-75750-3

The Cowboy's Triple Surprise

Copyright © 2017 by Barbara White-Rayczek

Printed in U.S.A.

Barbara White Daille and her husband still inhabit their own special corner of the wild, wild Southwest, where the summers are long and hot and the lizards and scorpions roam.

Barbara loves looking back at the short stories and two books she wrote in grade school and realizing that—except for the scorpions—she's doing exactly what she planned. She has now hit double digits with published novels and still has a file drawer full of stories to be written.

As always, Barbara hopes you will enjoy reading her books! She would love to have you drop by for a visit at her website, barbarawhitedaille.com.

Books by Barbara White Daille

Harlequin Western Romance

The Hitching Post Hotel

The Cowboy's Little Surprise
A Rancher of Her Own
The Lawman's Christmas Proposal
Cowboy in Charge

Harlequin American Romance

The Sheriff's Son
Court Me, Cowboy
Family Matters
A Rancher's Pride
The Rodeo Man's Daughter
Honorable Rancher
Rancher at Risk

Visit the Author Profile page
at Harlequin.com for more titles.

To Marlene and Vinnie
for the years of friendship,
fun, love and laughter...
and to Rich for all the same and more.

Chapter One

Tyler Buckham's life in Texas—though he wasn't sure you could call it a life lately—had become as dry as the Sonoran Desert. He liked the ranch he'd been working for some time now, and yet boredom and restlessness had both begun cropping up with increasing frequency. When he'd first noticed the signs setting in again, it never crossed his mind to turn to what he'd normally do: head out to another rodeo. Try for another prize. Find another buckle bunny to help fill a few empty hours.

That failure to go for what had always worked in the past proved just how stale his life had become.

As a last resort, he had given his notice and hit the road. Everybody needed a change of scenery once in a while. Running *to* something didn't have to mean you were running *from* something else. Or so he told himself.

With an effort, he brought his focus back to the den where he now sat, and looked at the older man across the desk from him. He had met Jed Garland, the owner of the Hitching Post Hotel, last summer, when he'd come to Garland Ranch to stand up as best man when Jed's granddaughter Tina married Tyler's friend Cole.

Jed laced his hands across his middle. "Nice to have you back."

"It's nice to be back," Tyler returned, though he felt uncomfortable saying it. He should have visited Cowboy Creek again long before this. Cole had invited him for Christmas, but he'd turned down the offer. Instead, he'd spent the holidays with his folks. Three months later, he was still kicking himself over that mistake.

"Cole will be pleased to see you when he gets home," Jed told him. "I'll need to have a talk with that boy, though—he didn't so much as hint about you coming for a visit."

"He didn't know I was headed this way. Stopping by was a spur-of-the-moment idea."

It was worse than that.

What would Cole and Jed and the rest of the Garlands think if they knew just how close he'd come to passing right by? Though he'd headed to New Mexico deliberately to put Texas behind him, he'd been on the fence about whether or not to visit Garland Ranch.

Fate had taken a hand, pushing him off the highway at the Cowboy Creek town limits. The gas gauge on the pickup had nose-dived, and he'd had to top up the tank. If he could have made it through to the next town, he might have left the hotel and dude ranch behind him in a cloud of road dust.

Instead, he'd given the truck its head the way he did his stallion. Like Freedom, the truck seemed to know exactly where it wanted to go. By the time he'd pulled into the parking area behind the Hitching Post, he had begun to wonder if fate had had this trip in store for him all along.

"Well," Jed said, "when an idea spurs you on, that's usually a good sign you should get moving on it."

"Yeah. And here I am." He glanced over at the Stetson he had tossed onto one of the small couches in the office. "But speaking of moving, I guess I'll hit the road again since Cole's not around."

"What's your hurry? He'll be back in a couple of days."

Tyler looked at Jed. The man was past seventy, but those clear blue eyes, topped by pure white eyebrows, wouldn't miss much. At Jed's scrutiny, he broke eye contact, using the excuse of grabbing his Stetson.

"It's almost time for lunch," Jed went on. "Why not stay to eat with us? Then you might as well stick around here till Cole gets home. We've got plenty of room in the hotel for you, and a stall out in the barn just standing empty waiting for your mount."

"I don't—"

"You know Tina and I will be glad for the visit with you," Jed went on, as if he hadn't heard Tyler. "And I know you're not planning on running off without seeing Paz."

The mention of Tina's grandmother, the hotel's cook, brought back some great memories. He smiled. "She sure took good care of me when I was here for Cole and Tina's wedding."

Jed smiled broadly. "Feeding people is what she does best. We don't like seeing anyone going hungry here. And we're not fond of empty spaces at the table. We'll be happy to have you sitting in for Cole and staying with us for a while."

"I don't—"

"You won't be the only guest at the table today," Jed broke in again. "Shay's joining us for lunch, too."

"Shay?" Tyler's pulse revved up a notch.

"Yeah, Shay O'Neill. You met her at the wedding last summer, remember?"

How could he forget? "Yeah, I remember Shay." Understatement of the century. The mention of her name brought to mind a handful of other good memories.

"So, that's decided." Jed rose from his chair. "C'mon out to the front desk and we'll find you a room. You haven't got much time to settle in before we eat. Just a word of advice, though. I'd do my best to show up in the dining room as soon as possible, or you might get done out of something special."

Yeah, something special like sitting next to Shay O'Neill.

As he followed Jed down the hall to the hotel lobby, his thoughts stayed with Shay. Shay, who was as sweet as the ice cream she sold at the Big Dipper in town. And who was way hotter than any other woman he'd ever seen.

Shay was another reason he should have come back to Cowboy Creek before now. They had had a good time in the few days he had stayed there last summer. No reason they couldn't have just as good a time while he was here now. Lucky for him, that brief visit had included a night in her bed. He looked forward to having that pleasure again.

Above all, Shay was guaranteed to make him forget his troubles for a while. He needed that kind of forgetting more than he'd realized until this very moment.

ONCE HE'D SETTLED Freedom in his stall, Tyler made quick work of hauling his duffel bag from the back of the pickup truck to the room Jed had assigned him. Minutes after tossing the bag onto the king-size bed, he was downstairs again and on his way to the dining room.

From up ahead, he could hear more than one conversation going, a child's shriek and, in a sudden beat of silence, a woman's familiar laugh. That last sound made him both hard and hungry, but not for anything the Hitching Post might serve for lunch.

The dining room was crowded with Garland family members and hotel guests, yet the instant he paused in the doorway, he spotted Shay. She sat on the far side of the long center table reserved for the Garlands, half turned away from him as she talked with one of Jed's granddaughters. He recognized the straight, wheat-blond hair that fell below her shoulders and felt like silk against his fingers. He knew when she looked his way he would see eyes one shade lighter than her green sweater. Her cheeks held a natural pink tint. Her lips curved in a soft smile.

Just looking at her from a distance made his pulse speed up and his jeans tighten.

She reached for a cloth napkin and unfolded it. As if she'd given a signal, the folks around him began heading toward the tables. The movement spurred him toward the vacant seat at her side before anyone else could grab it.

As he slid onto the chair, she turned his way.

The smile stayed, but the light pink color drained from her cheeks. He saw her fingers clutch the napkin she had draped across her lap. And then he saw the rounded expanse of belly straining the knitted weave of her sweater.

She was extremely pregnant.

Thoughts of anticipated pleasure flew from his head. Words did, too, leaving him struggling for something to say.

Jed Garland had no such problem. "Shay, you remember Tyler, don't you?"

She nodded.

"I thought you might."

Tyler couldn't tear his eyes away from her. He also couldn't miss hearing the satisfaction in the older man's voice. What had brought that on? And why had Jed mentioned Shay's invitation to lunch but said nothing about her condition? Of course, Jed—and everyone else at the Hitching Post—probably thought he and Shay were just passing acquaintances.

He tried for a casual smile. The one she gave him looked about as sincere as his felt.

"Tyler," Tina said, "Abuelo says you're staying with us for a while."

Shay's sweater rose, telling him she had sucked in a startled breath. She covered it with a small cough and a grab for her water glass.

The reaction made sense. Obviously, she'd met someone else since they were together last summer. Or she'd already been involved with the man when they'd had their fling. Either way, she wouldn't want him hanging around, maybe bringing up their brief relationship in some conversation. As if he would. The boys at the ranch back in Texas always said he needed to have "Love 'em and leave 'em" tattooed across his chest. That didn't mean he'd make a public announcement about a one-night stand. Shay couldn't know that, but you would think she'd at least give him the benefit of the doubt.

Finally dragging his gaze away, he turned to Tina.

He gave her his killer grin—to kill time, to try to pull himself together and recall what she had said... *Staying with us for a while.* Yeah. He sure regretted that right now. "I'll be here at least till Cole gets back. I wouldn't want to miss seeing him."

"He definitely wouldn't want to miss the opportunity, either. Meanwhile, we'll all have the pleasure of your company."

Not such a pleasure for Shay, considering the way she had reacted to finding him beside her and hearing he planned to stay. But that was nothing compared to the way he'd felt at seeing *her.*

Well...at seeing her *pregnant.*

While he liked a roll in the hay as well as any man, he had two rules for those occasions. First, always make sure your companion's unattached. Two, keep the relationship no strings. Obviously, he had let the first rule go by the wayside when he met Shay, but he sure intended to hold fast to the second.

Shay's condition now made him cross her name permanently off his interest list.

A waitress passed around several bowls filled with dinner rolls, then began serving the food. He managed to keep up his end of the conversation with Jed and Tina.

Shay apparently was making a deliberate effort to remain turned away from him as she talked to Jed's granddaughter Jane. Fine by him. The less they had to see of each other, the better. This lunch would soon be over, and considering the short time he planned to stay on the ranch, chances were good he wouldn't run into her again.

He passed the basket of rolls her way. As she took it from him, he glanced at her left hand. No chunky flashing diamonds, no gold band. And no surprise there. The boys he'd worked with had also filled him in about pregnant women. Namely, that toward the end of a pregnancy, they often gained too much weight to wear their wedding rings.

"Tyler?"

Abruptly, he became aware of Jed waving from the head of the table, attempting to get his attention. The man's tone made it apparent he'd said his name more than once. Flushing and hoping no one had noticed, he nodded at Jed in acknowledgment.

"If you haven't got any plans for the afternoon, the girls could use some help."

The girls meant Jed's adult granddaughters. "Sure. I've got nothing on my agenda." Besides avoiding Shay. "Need a hand with some heavy lifting?"

Jed nodded. "We're setting up for a wedding reception, and with Cole away, we're shorthanded around here. If you wouldn't mind going along to the banquet hall after lunch, maybe you can lend some assistance."

"No problem."

Jed beamed. "Thank you kindly. I appreciate it, and I know the girls and Shay all do, too."

"Shay?" he blurted, nearly dropping his fork.

To his relief, no one seemed to notice. Jed turned to talk to one of the hotel guests at an adjacent table. Tyler gripped his fork and tried not to look at the woman beside him.

He didn't feel comfortable being here with her. Judging by her white-knuckled grip on her water glass, she felt the same.

Things had definitely changed between them since the night they had spent together.

Chapter Two

After lunch, Shay hurried out of the dining room as quickly as she could, wanting to put distance between herself and Tyler. She gave a shuddering sigh and rested her hands on the small folding table she had set up near the entrance to the banquet room. The short walk here had left her unsteady on her feet, but for once she couldn't blame her shaky balance on the extra weight from her pregnancy.

She had never expected to see Tyler Buckham again, not after he'd left so many months before.

Eight months before. But who was counting?

In the short time he had been in Cowboy Creek last summer, she had fallen hard and fast for him. She had let just a few conversations over just a handful of days lead her to fall into his arms. And then she had made the awful mistake of taking him to bed.

The shame she felt about that now ranked right up there with the worst moments of her life, which included the day she finally acknowledged she wasn't going to hear from him again.

Now she had another item to add to the list— finding Tyler beside her an hour ago in the Hitching Post's dining room. Well, he wouldn't hear anything from her, either, about the fact he had gotten her pregnant before he'd left town.

"And he's not worth worrying about now, babies," she said under her breath. "Mommy needs to focus on the reason we're here at the Hitching Post."

The next wedding reception being held at the hotel was only a day away. And yet with all they still had left to do in the room, she had been demoted to assembling table decorations.

She had spread her supplies across the small table. On the far side of the room, Jane and a couple of the hotel's waitresses were taking care of the seating arrangements.

Truthfully, setting up chairs would almost be easier on her now than bending over the display cases at the Big Dipper to scoop up mounds of rock-solid ice cream. But she couldn't argue about being given light duty here, not when she knew the Garlands were only looking out for her.

Which was exactly what she needed to be doing right now for them.

She walked over to the corner of the room to get more of the wedding favors. Before she could lift the carton of vases from the stack, a man stepped up beside her. She nearly jumped a foot in the air.

Then she froze, knowing it was Tyler and refusing to look at him. Yet, without even a glance in his direction, she picked up so many of the same details she had tried not to notice at the dining room table. So many memories from their brief time together.

From the corner of her eye, she caught the scuffed and creased cowboy boots. The well-worn jeans. The snapped cuff of a long-sleeved Western shirt. With one breath, she took in the scent of musky aftershave and of the man himself. Standing so close to him, she couldn't miss the heat of his body. She forced herself to remember that warmth was only on the surface and didn't touch his heart.

"So," he said, "you're helping out the Garlands this afternoon, too?"

"I work here," she corrected.

"You gave up the job at the Big Dipper?"

She shook her head and finally glanced at him. "No, I'm doubling up. I'm working my way up to banquet manager for the hotel." She hoped for that, anyhow. With the babies on the way, she needed more money than she made now.

"Nice." He sounded impressed.

Good. Let him see she didn't need anything from him.

"Hey, I'll give you a hand." He grabbed the carton. Glass clinked.

"Careful," she snapped, half out of annoyance at herself for taking so much of him in, the other half out of irritation at his thinking she needed help—or anything else—from him. "Those are fragile."

Eyebrows raised, he eyed her middle as if to say the same applied to her.

She crossed her arms, intending to stand her ground and stare him down, but the large baby bump made the stance awkward. She lowered her hands to her sides.

"Don't worry," he said, "I don't make a habit of dropping things."

"Oh, really? I'd have said you were an expert at it." She could have bitten her tongue at the instinctive response, but even that pain wouldn't have come close to the way he had hurt her.

"What does that mean?"

It was too much to hope he would have just let her statement slide. But why should she let *him* slide when he had treated her so badly? "Sorry. I suppose I shouldn't have said that." She kept her voice down, but still, nerves and anger made her pitch high and her tone arch. "I really don't know how you are about dropping *things*. But I sure know how you are about dropping *women*, since you did such a great job of that with me."

Abruptly, he shifted the carton. Glass clinked again, and this time she was too annoyed to care. How could he sound so offhand after what he had done?

"I didn't drop you," he said. "You knew I was only in town a few days for the wedding. While I was here, we had a good time together, and that was it. I didn't make any promises." He looked at her stomach. "Besides, you obviously didn't waste any time moving on to someone else."

She swallowed a gasp. He couldn't possibly think she had slept with him one night and then gone on to someone else the next. Then again, considering how quickly she had wound up in bed with him, why wouldn't he think that?

As for not wasting time... If he only knew how many sleepless nights she had spent since he had left, especially once she found out she was pregnant. But he wouldn't know, and she had to stop thinking about that. He had already stolen too much time from her, had already hurt her enough.

"Don't worry," he said in a lower tone, "I'm not planning to say anything about what happened last summer. Your secret's safe with me."

"My—" The sound of footsteps made her cut herself off. This time she turned. One sneak attack was enough—although no one could have startled her more than Tyler had.

Tina was coming toward them from across the room.

Shay glanced in Tyler's direction and gestured to the table she had set up. "You can put the carton over there. Thanks." She forced a smile.

He locked gazes with her. She refused to be the first to look away, which left her staring into his midnight-blue eyes. To her dismay, her stomach did that funny little flip it had taken such a short time to learn months ago.

"Tyler," Tina said, "thanks so much for agreeing to help us all out. I think Jane's trying to flag you down. Would you mind giving her and the waitresses a hand with the banquet tables?"

"Sure." He glanced toward the other side of the room. Then he nodded to them both and ambled away.

Shay tried not to stare after him. She didn't care where he was going or what he was doing, as long as it wasn't near her. Let him think what he wanted about her pregnancy, too. She didn't have to correct his assumption.

"Shay?"

Startled, she turned to stare at Tina. "I'm sorry. What?"

"I said, why don't you sit and take it easy? It's hard to be up on your feet, especially when you can't even *see* your feet."

"You should talk," Shay said, glancing pointedly at the other woman's middle, then blinking as she recalled Tyler doing the same to her. "You're not that far behind me."

"But I'm experienced. And I'm not carrying three babies."

Shay tried not to wince, not to react at all to what Tina had said. She shot another look across the banquet hall. To her relief, Tyler had reached the opposite side of the room. Even with the acoustics in the high-ceilinged ballroom, he couldn't possibly have overheard.

"Actually," Tina said, "I'll give you a hand, since I have some free time this afternoon." She took a seat at the table.

Shay followed and returned to her own chair. Again, she couldn't argue. Tina was only looking out for her. And as one of the Garland family, the other woman was more or less her employer.

She didn't know what Tyler was doing back here in Cowboy Creek, but for all she knew, Jed might have hired him, too. She might have to face him every time she came to the hotel to work.

The thought was too much for her to consider.

She reached for the ribbon dispenser. Right now, she needed to push aside her reluctance to be near him for even part of this afternoon. She had to focus on the job that was going to help her pay her bills.

And still, she stared across the room.

Tyler had gone down on one knee to inspect something under a table. His broad shoulders strained against his flannel shirt the way her stomach strained against her maternity top. His belt encircled a waist as rock hard as his abs and now slimmer than she was around the middle.

"Shay," Tina said, "do you mind if I borrow that dispenser before you run out of ribbon?"

Shay looked down at the table in front of her. Her

face flamed. While trying to distract her thoughts from Tyler, she had coiled a length of ribbon into a tangled mass around her fingers. She grabbed the scissors and snipped the ribbon free.

Without another word, Tina took the dispenser, then reached for an undecorated vase. Shay sent her an apologetic glance, but the other woman didn't look her way.

For a while, she managed to focus on the vases and the ribbons and a casual conversation with Tina. Then, all too soon, she found herself tuning in to the thump of Tyler's boots from the other side of the room, the rumble of his voice as he spoke to one of the women, the sound of his deep laugh as he responded to something one of them said.

A spurt of jealousy hit, an unwanted, unwelcome emotion that twined itself—like the ribbon twisted in her fingers—around her heart.

She should have expected it and been prepared. And she couldn't let it worry her, because she knew what caused the sudden upswing of emotion.

From the day Tyler had left to the day she finally acknowledged he didn't plan to contact her again, her up-and-down feelings had run out of control. Late-night anxiety triggered her bouts of insomnia. Stiff-necked tension left her no comfortable position even if sleep had wanted to come. Anger and depression had made her days as uncomfortable as her nights.

There had been no way she would have run after Tyler, no way she wanted an unreliable cowboy in her life. Anger at herself, at how far she had let herself fall, had triggered every one of those reactions. She had simply waited them out, knowing they would pass, and they had. Eventually.

After she had discovered she was pregnant, she had again fought—and won—a battle to get her emotions in check, but there were times, like today, when her hormones won out. Green-eyed jealousy was trying to entice her. She wouldn't let it succeed. Tyler didn't mean anything to her anymore. She couldn't care less who he flirted with now. Though he had fathered her babies, he was a free man.

She didn't plan to do or say anything to change that.

WHEN HIS YOUNGEST GRANDDAUGHTER, Tina, entered the kitchen, Jed Garland took notice. Her grin made him sit back in his chair and nod in satisfaction.

Paz, standing near the refrigerator, stopped and turned their way.

"Tyler went for the bait, did he?" Jed asked.

"I don't know about that." Tina laughed. "But as you would put it, let's just say Jane had him well and truly hooked by the time I left the banquet hall. He's helping with the table setups, though his attention keeps wandering, and so does Shay's. I'm now beginning to think you were right all along. You're some matchmaker, Abuelo."

"I try," he said modestly.

Both she and Paz laughed out loud.

"I'm curious," Tina said. "Tyler seemed so reluctant to help after you told him Shay would be working with us. I'm surprised he's cooperating now. What did you say to him after the rest of us left the dining room?"

"I simply mentioned that no able-bodied man would let a woman in Shay's condition get overworked."

"Mentioned?" Paz repeated.

Chuckling, he looked over at the hotel cook. She had

worked for him for more than twenty years now, since before they had this granddaughter in common and long before those gray streaks had started threading through her hair. "Well, maybe a bit stronger than mentioned. What do *you* think of his reaction?"

She crossed the room to take the chair beside Tina's. After a glance toward the kitchen door, she smiled at them both. "I think it has proved your point. If we didn't already believe that Tyler is the daddy of Shay's babies, I would surely think so now."

He nodded. "We'd have had to be imbeciles not to have caught on months ago. The boy's reactions today only confirm he and Shay had something going on."

"True," Tina said. "I was watching, and the look on his face when he stood in the doorway and saw her was priceless. So was Shay's when she found him sitting beside her. But I'm feeling a little guilty you didn't tell either of them ahead of time that they would see each other at lunch."

He shook his head. "There's a lot to be said for shock value. And there's even more to be said about keeping those two on their toes. Jane and the other girls are still with them in the banquet hall, aren't they?"

Tina nodded.

"Good. Nothing like holding something a man wants within his sight but just out of reach. I'm betting the longer he has time to question things, the more eager he'll be to stick around to get answers. And in the long run, the more Shay will benefit."

"Yes." Paz nodded. "We have to think of Shay."

"We do," he agreed. "It's best we all pretend ignorance for as long as we can. Then they'll never suspect we're trying to get them together."

"You think this plan is a good one, Jed?" Paz asked.

"Of course, I do. And it's not just me and the girls who believe in it."

Tina gasped. "You talked to Mo?"

"I did, just before lunch. And she's in complete agreement. Shay puts on a good act when she's with any of us, but her grandma said she's been moping for months now at home. And that's not good for her."

"Especially in her condition," Paz said in alarm.

"Exactly. Well, don't worry. We'll be keeping her much too busy to worry about anything…except Tyler."

"You are a devious, scheming man," she said, shaking her head.

"Thank you," he said with a grin.

Chapter Three

"We need that table over here," Jane called across the banquet room.

"No problem." Tyler turned in midstride, rolling the round table on its edge across the hardwood floor toward the space she indicated. "You ladies sure do know how to put a man to work around here."

"Are you complaining?"

"Heck, no. Hard labor is my middle name." Though Jane laughed, he couldn't keep from wincing. Head down, he busied himself with pulling out the legs of the table and tightening the supports. Then he crossed back to the wheeled cart and took down the next table.

The phrase he'd jokingly tossed out—*hard labor*—had made him think of Shay and her pregnancy. Where was the man who had gotten her into that state? There had to be someone in the vicinity. A husband. A boyfriend. Someone. Despite her lack of a wedding ring, for all he knew, she had married that someone a week after he had left town.

It looked to him as though she might be ready to have her baby at any minute. But what did he know about that, either? After lunch, she had stood from her seat beside his and lumbered away. Except for the rolling gait of a saddle-sore greenhorn, from the back she seemed just the way she had when he'd met her months ago. Quite a few months ago.

For a moment, his thoughts got hung up on the time frame. But only for a moment. He couldn't have been the one to get her pregnant. After all, when he had said something about her moving on to someone else as soon as he'd left town, she hadn't denied it.

"Hold up, Tyler," Jane called. "The reception's in this room, not on the patio."

To his chagrin, he saw he'd overshot his mark and was almost to a pair of doors leading outside. "Got it," he said, forcing a laugh. Abruptly, he turned back and took the table to the appropriate spot.

As he continued to work, Shay remained absorbed in her vases and ribbons. Every time he attempted to set up a table closer to her, Jane sent him to another area of the room.

Maybe that was for the best. He and Shay didn't have anything left to say to each other. And they couldn't have talked much, anyway, with Tina or Jane constantly by her side. It was as if they were standing guard over her. Every time Jed stopped by the room, even he seemed to take up a protective stance. Because...

Because she *was* due to have that baby at any minute?

Despite his own reassurances to himself, he did some quick mental math. The results caused him to pull his bandanna from his back pocket. It took him two tries to wipe the cold sweat from his face.

"You okay, cowboy?" Jane called teasingly.

Across the room, Shay looked up from her work.

"Ma'am," he said to Jane, "I've had a change of heart. You're about working me to death here." He grinned.

"Even the hired hands ought to be entitled to a cold drink now and then, don't you think?"

He saw her fighting to hide a smile. She made a show of glancing at her watch. "Well, I suppose we can spare you for a minute."

"Good." He ambled across the room, deliberately avoiding Shay and Tina and aiming straight for the corner table a few yards from them. Earlier, one of the waitresses had brought in a jug of sweet tea. He filled a glass.

After a mouthful of the drink, he turned to look at the two women. Both were pregnant. Was there something in the water around here? He eyed his tea glass and swallowed a laugh. Then he looked at Shay's belly again, and his sense of humor deserted him.

He needed to act normally around her, as though he didn't have a care in the world. Which he didn't. Hoping for a casual approach, he headed toward their table. From across the room he saw Jane start their way, too.

He came to a stop beside Shay, not too near, but close enough to see the long sweep of her lashes as she kept her eyes down, her gaze focused on her work. Close enough to smell the same flowery perfume she had worn last summer when he'd danced with her at the wedding and, a few nights later, when he had slept with her in her bed.

He gulped another mouthful of sweet tea and nearly choked on it.

Shay never looked his way. The chances she would even throw a glance at him seemed less likely by the second. That only made him more determined to get her attention. He gestured toward the vases lined up on the table. "Looks like this is going to be one big wedding."

He stood facing Shay, but Tina answered instead. "The biggest we've had here yet," she said emphatically.

He knew she was the financial genius in the family. "The thought of all that income must make your accountant's heart beat faster."

She laughed. "You must have heard that phrase from Cole."

"I did." He looked at Shay. Another, more intimate memory of them together flashed into his mind. "What makes *your* heart speed up?" he blurted.

"Heartburn," she said flatly.

He blinked. Maybe that was a symptom of pregnancy. Or maybe she was just pulling his leg.

"*This* worker is due for a break, too," she said, bracing her hands on the table. She seemed to have trouble pushing herself to her feet. Afraid she might overbalance and fall over the chair, he held it steady for her just as he'd done in the dining room after lunch. And just like then, she gave him a curt, dismissive nod. "Tina, I'm going for a walk. I'll be back in a few minutes."

"Good idea," he said. "I feel the need to stretch my legs, too."

Her eyes narrowed. "You're not—"

"—thinking of leaving us, are you?" Tina finished. "Tyler, I'm surprised at you. We've still got so many tables to set up."

"We certainly do," Jane said. "And we've run into a little problem over there." She pointed to the far side of the room. She raised her brows.

Tina smiled.

Shay turned and left the room.

Shrugging, he followed Jane across the banquet hall.

He'd been roped into helping again, and danged if he could think of a single good excuse that would cut him loose.

Somehow, he managed to carry on a conversation with Jane and the rest of the women while his brain focused on the topic of Shay's baby. The first chance he had to find her alone, he wanted an answer to the question that continued to nag at him:

Just how far along is *she?*

FOR THE REST of the afternoon, Jane kept him hopping. The closest Tyler got to Shay was when he set up chairs at the tables in the area near where she was working.

He had just come within yards of her when she pulled a cell phone from the bag she had hooked over the back of her chair. After checking the display, she turned to Tina. "I need another break. And I missed a call from my grandmother."

"Give Mo our regards," Tina said.

Shay nodded. This time she appeared to have less trouble getting up. She also seemed to be in a hurry, as if she wanted to get out of her seat before he could lend his help.

He watched her walk off.

A few minutes later, Tina left the ballroom, too.

Time ticked away, and neither of the women returned.

Eventually, Jed and Paz stopped in the doorway and surveyed the setup. Tyler tucked the final two chairs beneath a table, then sauntered in their direction.

"Looking good," Jed said.

Tyler eyed the room and tried to see it from the older man's perspective. All the tables had been covered with long white cloths and shorter pale blue ones, but only half the sets of silverware wrapped in white napkins had been put in place. And there were no decorations around the room yet.

He gestured to the folding table at which Shay and Tina had been sitting. "Looks like two of your helpers have deserted you."

"Tina had to go back to work in her office," Paz said.

"And Shay left," Jed put in, answering Tyler's unspoken question.

"Left?" he asked, startled. Then he backpedaled, trying to downplay his interest. "I mean, I thought she was in charge of table decorations."

"She is. But she got a call from her grandma and said she had to go home."

Jed made the statement so calmly, Tyler couldn't jump to the conclusion that anything was wrong. He also couldn't keep from wondering whether Shay had wanted to avoid him. At that thought, the hairs on the back of his neck stood at attention. She had no reason to stay away from him now. He'd assured her he wouldn't bring up their past.

He thought back to Cole and Tina's wedding and what had happened a couple of days after, and couldn't help rechecking his math. But even if the dates tallied, that didn't have to mean a thing. They'd seen each other less than a handful of times. They'd slept together once. What were the chances she'd gotten pregnant from what amounted to a one-night stand? A heck of a lot slimmer than her waist right now, that was sure.

He focused on his surroundings again and found Paz looking his way. If he didn't know better, he'd swear he saw sympathy in her gaze.

"Shay told me to tell Jed she was sorry," she explained. "Her grandmother is fine. I think it was Shay who wasn't feeling well. Tina will call her in a little while to make sure she arrived home."

"Good idea." Jed nodded.

"If she felt that sick," Tyler said, "you'd think she'd have called her husband to pick her up."

"Doesn't have a husband," Jed returned.

"No *novio*—boyfriend—either," Paz added.

Exactly the question Tyler's mental mathematics had caused him to consider all afternoon. But asking Jed or Paz about Shay's pregnancy would only bring more unwanted attention to his interest in a woman he should only barely know.

SHAY STRETCHED OUT on her friend's couch, putting her tired feet up in hopes of easing the swelling. She pulled the afghan from the back of the couch and spread it over her, but even the weight of the knitted wool couldn't banish the chill she felt.

Layne came from the apartment's small kitchen carrying a tray with a couple of mugs and a plate of cookies. When she held out one of the steaming mugs, Shay took it gratefully.

Though she hadn't eaten much of her lunch at the Hitching Post, she couldn't even look at the cookies. When she got home, she would have to have something. Not now. The way her stomach felt at the moment, she almost didn't want to risk a sip of tea, either. But she needed the warmth. Needed the mug to hold on to.

She sighed again and glanced at Layne, the only person who knew the truth about her pregnancy. "Tyler's going to figure out the timing, if he hasn't already. Even if he's not the type to keep track of dates—" *or to keep track of his conquests* "—he'll remember the month of the wedding. So many brides get married in June."

As if to challenge that tradition, Layne and her ex-husband had remarried at the Hitching Post just this past weekend.

Shortly before that, Jed's widowed granddaughter, Andi, had gotten married, too. Those newlyweds were still away on their honeymoon.

Like Tina, Shay had always dreamed of a June wedding and lots of children. Her dreams never included having those children first or raising a family on her own.

But she wouldn't be alone. She had Grandma and Layne and the Garlands, and the rest of her friends. They were all she needed. All her babies needed, too.

"He'll figure it out," she said again. "Or maybe someone at the Hitching Post already told him my due date."

"Is that so bad?" Layne asked quietly. "You're going to tell him, anyway, aren't you?"

"No, I'm not." A flash of anger left her breathless. But it was fury at her own actions that caused tears to rise beneath her hurt. What a fool she had been to fall for Tyler's dark good looks, his great pickup lines and his pretense of genuine interest. Well, he *had* truly been interested in something, anyhow. In getting her into bed. And she had made it all too easy for him. She tightened her fingers around the mug. "He slept with me—once—and never looked back. Why would I chase after him to tell him the news?"

"Because he's the father."

"No, he's not."

Layne's eyes opened so wide, Shay couldn't help but laugh. Then, sobering, she slumped against the couch cushion. "Of course he's the father. I don't…"

I don't sleep around. But she had. One single time.

She glanced across the living room to where Layne's little girl lay sleeping in her playpen. Layne's new husband had left a few minutes ago, taking their son into the kids' room to read him a story.

"Don't worry," Layne said, "they'll be good for an hour or more."

Shay nodded. Still, she lowered her voice, as much out of reluctance to confess the truth as from the worry she would be overheard. "I only meant that Tyler wouldn't be a real father. How could he be? And why would I *want* him to be, when he didn't care enough about me to come back again, or even to call or send me a text?"

"You don't know what happened after he left."

"I don't want to know," she said flatly. "I don't want to know anything more than I do already—that he was so hot and such a sweet-talker. And I was such easy pickings."

"Don't say that."

"Why not? You know it. I know it. And worst of all, he knows it, too."

"I know *you*, Shay. You wouldn't have slept with him if you didn't care about him."

"I can't believe this." She stared down at her tea. "At the wedding, the two of us just clicked."

"I know you did."

As the groom's sister, Layne had attended the wedding last summer, too. At the reception, she had witnessed Shay's first meeting with Tyler. So had almost everyone else in Cowboy Creek. "The day after the wedding," Shay said slowly, "he came to the Big Dipper with Jane and Pete and the kids. He came back *every* day. He borrowed a truck from Jed."

She had already told Layne all that, but not the rest. "The night before he planned to leave, he showed up again. It was so beautiful out, and after I closed up the shop we went for a walk. We wound up at my house and…and Grandma was out at her bridge club. And I guess you can figure out the rest." She blinked. "I didn't plan it."

"But you wanted it to happen," Layne said softly.

Shay nodded.

"Because you cared. And because you thought he cared about you."

"Yes." She shrugged. "What difference does it make what I thought? Obviously, I was wrong." At least, on one of those counts. "And how can I ever face him again?"

"He's not just passing through?"

She shook her head. "Oh, I'm sure he'll be leaving soon enough. But…"

"But he came to see Cole," Layne guessed. "And Cole's gone to Denver to check out that new stallion for Jed."

"Right. Tyler's staying until he gets back. And I've got to go to work at the Hitching Post again. We've got the wedding tomorrow night." She winced, filled with guilt about the way she had sent along an apology with Paz earlier, and then escaped from the hotel.

Still, she couldn't regret leaving. The Hitching Post was *not* the place for a reunion with Tyler. She'd needed to get away. Needed to get some space while she figured out how to do what she knew she had to do. Tell him the truth about her pregnancy.

She had to tell him about the children she would soon be having. Not one child. Not two. But three small, unexpected babies, already growing and thriving inside her. Already very much loved.

Not his babies.

Hers.

"How did you get away from the hotel today without having to talk to Tyler?" Layne asked.

Shay explained about the missed phone call, which she had noticed on her cell phone at the best possible time. "Grandma just wanted to remind me not to hurry home, since she had plans to be out for supper at Sugar-Pie's." The sandwich shop in town was one of Mo's favorite hangouts, and Sugar Conway, the owner, was one of her best friends. "It gave me a reason to leave the banquet room. Once I was away from everyone," she confessed, "I used the call as an excuse to run. Which is going to make going back tomorrow even more awkward."

"Couldn't you just call in sick?" Layne asked.

She almost choked on a laugh. "I wish. But I can't let Jed and everyone else down. Besides, I need the money. Neither of my part-time jobs comes with insurance."

"I thought you told me you had money from your parents."

"I do. From their life insurance policies. So at least I won't have to worry about the hospital bills."

She didn't want to think about those policies and what they represented—the mom and dad she had lost years ago. Money couldn't take their place in her life. But in reality, she had lost them both long before the accident that had taken them away. Her dad had chased the rodeo and her mom had chased her dad, and as a result, she had never really had them in her life to begin with. All the more reason for staying away from Tyler.

How could she have let herself...

How could she have *slept* with a rodeo cowboy?

"Grandma practically raised me," she said in a low voice. "I know how much she loves me, and I know she'll help me out. But I'm trying to save up as much as I can for everything else the babies will need. I *have* to report to the Hitching Post tomorrow."

She looked at Layne. "But I'm just dreading having to walk back into that hotel and see Tyler again. Or having to face any of the Garlands. Everyone else in Cowboy Creek must know the situation, too. What did I think?" she added, rolling her eyes. "That I could hide my head in the sand like an ostrich, and they wouldn't figure out the timing as soon as they saw my stomach getting bigger?"

Layne smothered a laugh. "Sorry. That's some visual. But if hiding the truth was your goal, I'm afraid you can forget it. Take it from a mom twice over. Nobody around here messes up the math on a pregnancy." Sobering, she added, "I know you don't want to tell Tyler the news, Shay. But you should think about it. Before someone else does."

"People ought to respect my right to privacy," she snapped.

"In *this* town? No. Someone, sometime, is bound to tell him—out of the goodness of their heart, though. You know that."

"Oh, I do know. They'll have the best of motives, thinking they're making things easier and doing me a favor."

"Exactly. The longer you wait, the more you run that risk. And worse, the more gossip and speculation will fly."

"I know that, too," she mumbled. Her eyes blurring, she stroked her stomach and sighed.

Chapter Four

Tyler patted the stallion's flank, then left the stall.

In the corral outside the barn, a few of the hotel guests were saddled up, looking stiff and serious as they took instruction from some of the cowhands.

He headed across the yard to the Hitching Post.

The wind had picked up a bit, but the midafternoon sun had gotten stronger. Together, they kept the temperature at a comfortable level. Too bad they couldn't do anything about *his* temperature. Since yesterday, he had jumped from hot to cold and back again every time he thought of Shay.

As he reached the hotel, the back door opened. Pete, Jed's ranch manager and Jane's husband, came out of the hotel and down the porch steps. "In for the day?" he asked.

Tyler nodded.

"Whenever you're needing another ride, you're welcome to any of the mounts here."

"Needing?" Tyler echoed.

Pete shrugged. "The way you tore out of here after lunch, I'd have said you were looking for more than just time in the saddle."

"Yeah." All morning, he had helped Tina and Jane

in the ballroom again. Shay hadn't been around, and no one had mentioned her name.

They had released him from duty just before lunch, and afterward he and Freedom had done some hard riding on Garland Ranch. The long trek had been designed to help him outrun his thoughts. Instead, it had only given him more time alone, ample time to envision what he'd seen yesterday.

Shay, with her belly so big she looked like she might give birth at any moment. Not that he was an expert on pregnancy. But he could count. And he still didn't like the numbers he'd come up with.

"The ride doesn't seem to have done you much good," Pete said. "Or else that expression of yours is saying you hit a cactus patch somewhere out on the ranch."

"I hit something thorny," he agreed, wondering just how much the other man could help him. Pete had two kids of his own. He certainly ought to know something about the stages of pregnancy. He might also know when Shay was due to have her baby.

But he didn't intend to stand there gossiping about her with Jed's ranch manager. Or even to discuss her with Jed. He had to talk to Shay. All day, he'd replayed their conversation in his mind. Her lack of reaction when he had said he would keep her secret told him he couldn't be the daddy. But he needed her to tell him herself.

"See you later." Tyler made his way into the Hitching Post. A short walk down the hall took him to the wide doorway of the hotel's kitchen.

Paz stood near a counter, where light glinted off a knife resting on a cutting board filled with raw vegetables. She broke off from what she was saying to gesture toward a large coffeemaker on one counter. "Coffee is brewed there."

"Thanks."

At the large table, Jed sat with a mug in front of him. "Take a load off," he invited, waving at an empty chair.

Tyler filled a mug and took his seat at the table.

"As I was saying," Paz said to Jed, "Tina talked with Shay and told her we won't need her for the reception tonight. Shay's planning to work at the shop instead, but she said she'll be here tomorrow afternoon."

"Good."

Not so good for him. Tomorrow afternoon seemed a long time away. And if the Garlands herded her like a stray mare again, chances were good he probably wouldn't get to talk to her alone. He couldn't let this opportunity pass him by. "Shay seems to be pretty far along."

"She is," Paz confirmed. "She has just a few weeks left."

"We're trying to keep her from overdoing it," Jed put in. "That's why we appreciated your help yesterday and this morning. You deserved the break after lunch. Enjoy your ride?"

"Yeah," he said, not satisfied with changing the subject but unwilling to push the issue. "It felt good to get out."

"Of the hotel?"

"Just out. On horseback." What had those all-knowing blue eyes seen to make Jed ask that question? He couldn't tell the man the truth.

Last night, he had spent the evening with the Garlands and their hotel guests. And yeah, between that and today's stint in the ballroom, then at the crowded lunch table, he *had* felt the need to get out of the hotel, to get away on his own. To put some space between him and the Garland family. Along with Jed and Paz, and not counting the absent newlyweds, that included two granddaughters, one of their husbands and a handful of kids. A lot of Garlands to go around. He'd needed some breathing room.

Maybe it was having all the other hotel guests there, too, that left him feeling boxed in. Maybe it was just the fact he'd grown up without brothers or sisters and had gotten used to the quiet.

But mostly, he suspected it had to do with needing to escape his thoughts of Shay. Like that had worked.

"Cole ought to be back tomorrow," Jed said.

"Good. I'm looking forward to seeing him." Heck, he needed the diversion. "He's flying in from Denver?"

"Driving. He was making a couple of stops along the way." Jed took another sip of coffee. "Paz and I were just talking about you before you walked in."

"Me? What's up?"

"With this reception going on, we're all going to be tied up most of the evening. I'm afraid you'll be on your own."

"No problem. I'm sure I can find something—" *or someone* "—to keep me occupied."

SHAY SLID THE decorated cake into the large freezer in the Big Dipper's workroom. Their ice cream cakes were always in demand for birthdays and other celebrations. And though SugarPie's bakery supplied the wedding and party cakes for the Hitching Post, the Dipper always took care of the hotel's ice cream orders.

She didn't want to think about the hotel or about the

man she had last seen there yesterday. She touched her stomach. "I probably should have stayed to talk to him," she murmured to her babies, "but the two of us were never alone." She laughed softly. "And I don't mean because *you* three were there with me." She sobered again. The thought of having her conversation with Tyler in front of any of the Garlands had done her in, making her run at the first opportunity.

With a sigh, she closed the freezer door securely, then returned to the empty front room of the shop.

They did a booming business in the warmer months, good enough for her boss to pay her a decent wage all year round. Unfortunately, the job was only part-time. As she had told Layne, she needed her income from the Hitching Post, where they paid her an even better part-time rate.

As if the thought of Layne had summoned her, the door to the shop opened and she stepped inside.

"What brings you here?" Shay asked in surprise.

"A pint of chocolate-marshmallow swirl, for one thing."

"You're not pregnant again, are you?"

Layne laughed. "That's what Jason asked. No, I'm not. But the craving was a good reason to get me over here." She went to the small freezer off to one side of the room.

"Like you need a reason for ice cream." Shay leaned against the counter instead of taking the high stool out from beneath it. She didn't trust herself on the stool. After growing so much in the past few weeks, she was finding it harder to keep her balance even with her feet flat on the floor.

Layne set her container on the counter. After looking

around the still-empty shop, she said, "I stopped in at the L-G to pick up a few groceries this afternoon and ran into Mo. We had quite a chat."

The look of excitement on Layne's face made Shay blink in surprise. "A chat about what?"

"Your hours."

Again, Shay blinked. Her hours wouldn't have given anyone reason to feel excited…unless Grandma had heard something from Jed about giving her more work time.

"Mo told me you were here tonight and not helping out at the Hitching Post."

"Oh. That." Usually, she waitressed at the receptions and parties.

"Yes, that. What did you think we talked about? What happened?"

"I don't know for sure. Tina called earlier today and told me they wouldn't need me for the reception. They're probably worried I'll go into labor in the middle of the dance floor."

Layne laughed. "You know that's not it."

"Well, maybe not." She shrugged. "She did say Jed wants me to come out to the Hitching Post tomorrow afternoon. I hope he's planning to give me more hours." Or a raise.

"I hope so, too, at least until it's time for you to stay off your feet. Which is getting close, isn't it?"

"Don't you start, too. I saw Dr. Grayden Thursday morning. The babies are doing fine, and he said I'm still good to go with the date we've scheduled for my C-section. And he and my specialist in Santa Fe gave me their okay to continue working."

"With no restrictions?"

"I just have to take things easy," she admitted.

"We all realize that. So remember, if Jed doesn't offer you as many extra hours as you'd like, it's because everybody out at the ranch is concerned about you."

"You could have fooled me," Shay said as she rang up the purchase. "Jed might be, but Tina and Jane spent more time falling all over Tyler than they did watching out for me. I was glad they kept him occupied—and away from me." They had kept him busy on the other side of the room, except for that short time he had stood next to her. She had continued working, had forced herself not to look up, yet she had been as aware of him as if he'd plopped himself down in the center of all the vases on the table in front of her.

"Have you decided what you're going to do about talking to him?" Layne asked.

"Not yet." Sighing, she scooped up the pile of pennies in the cash register drawer and let them trickle through her fingers. "I know you're right. If I don't tell him, someone else will. But I want to do it my way. In my own time."

"Which still means not at all," Layne said wryly. "Otherwise, you would have managed to talk to him at the ranch yesterday."

Shay reached for the twenty-dollar bill Layne held out. "I couldn't have, with everyone around."

"That makes sense. With news like yours to share, you're going to need some time alone with him."

Her insides turned as cold as a tub of ice cream. It had nothing to do with the freezer case beside her and everything to do with the picture Layne's words had formed in her mind. "At the rate things are going, it doesn't seem likely that's going to happen."

But even as she said the words, she knew she was going to have to *make* it likely. No matter how she felt about Tyler, he was going to have to learn the truth. And *she* wanted to be the one to break the news to him.

The one to tell him he had gotten her pregnant, and she didn't want him anywhere near her or her kids.

As she handed Layne the change, she saw, beyond her, a customer standing outside the glass-paned front door. She curled her fingers against her empty palm and swallowed a groan of frustration.

Tyler swung the door open. When he stepped into the shop, the temperature suddenly seemed to rise by a hundred degrees.

He nodded at her and removed his Stetson.

Layne looked toward the door. "Well, hi there. It's been a while."

"Yeah, it has."

Layne said something else; Tyler replied. Shay saw their mouths moving, but panic seemed to have closed her ears.

"Well." Layne turned and sent Shay a sympathetic glance as she reached for the sack with her ice cream. "I'd better get home before this melts," she said brightly. In a lower voice, she said, "Good luck with your private chat."

Not here. Not now. "You don't have to go," she protested just as Tyler opened the door again. For a moment, she held on to the hope he planned to leave. But he was only being polite for Layne.

Too bad he hadn't been a gentleman for her.

She flushed, knowing she was at least half to blame for winding up...*together* with him. At least half to blame, if not much more, for believing in something that wasn't meant to be.

He closed the door behind Layne and turned Shay's way.

The room seemed to spin—not a symptom of pregnancy she had experienced before. She put her hands on the counter in front of her. "Don't tell me they've sent you here from the Hitching Post for ice cream." She fought to keep her voice steady. "I happen to know what's on the menu for the reception tonight, and everything's covered."

"Nobody sent me here. But everyone's all tied up, and I had time on my hands."

"Really? You didn't have Jed to talk to?"

"He said he'd be busy all night at the reception."

She frowned. "That's strange. He always makes an appearance, but he's never stayed the entire time, except at his granddaughters' weddings. Well, then, what about Pete?" Jane and her husband lived in the manager's house on Garland Ranch. "And if he's busy, you've got plenty of cowhands to hang out with."

"Maybe I had the urge for dessert."

"Then you'll find more of a selection at SugarPie's."

"Could be. But maybe what I want's right here."

Once she would have fallen for that line and hoped he wanted *her*. She was so over that now. So over him.

She slid open the freezer case and pulled out an empty ice cream tub. It gave her the excuse to walk away, to go into the workroom and avoid his blue-eyed stare. Shaking her head in disgust at herself, she crossed to the big freezer.

She had been all too good at analyzing his expression these past couple of days. She had seen the surprise on his face after he noticed the size of her stomach, had witnessed his frustration as she stood to leave the banquet hall. And just a minute ago, she had clearly read the determination in his eyes.

As she pulled open the freezer door, cold air blasted her. With luck, it would shock some sense into her. Hands shaking, she reached up to the top shelf for another tub of butter-pecan ice cream.

Just as he had yesterday, Tyler stepped up beside her. Again, she nearly jumped out of her shoes.

"I'll get it." He grabbed the tub she intended to take off the shelf.

"Thanks, but I'm pregnant, not incapacitated."

"I didn't think you were." He slammed the freezer door shut. "Let's just say I'll scratch your back, you scratch mine."

The image that followed his words stole her breath.

He looked away, as if he'd only now realized what he had said. He cleared his throat and looked back at her. "I'll take care of this, then you can take care of a few things for me."

Unfortunately, his attempt to make his point clearer only filled her mind with bittersweet images and memories. Tyler flirting with her at Cole and Tina's reception... Tyler's hand brushing hers as they walked the streets of Cowboy Creek on a moonlit night... Tyler kissing her thoroughly as he ran his fingers through her hair...

She had to get her thoughts and this conversation back on track. "Take care of a few things?" she repeated.

"Questions."

This close, he seemed to tower over her. It wasn't a

menacing stance, just a result of the difference in their heights. She had grown up as one of the tallest girls in school, and after meeting Tyler at the wedding, she had liked that he made her feel petite. She still liked it. His towering didn't bother her.

It was his nearness that left her feeling shaky. This close and at this stage in her pregnancy, her rounded stomach nearly brushed his flat abs. This close, she could see every darker fleck in his dark blue eyes, making her wonder if any of her babies would have eyes the same shade.

She didn't move. He didn't, either. After a moment she realized she stood leaning back against the freezer door. The cool metal sent another shiver through her. The cold tub he held in one arm, so close to her, added to her chill.

And still, they stood as frozen as two ice cream sandwiches.

Finally, she tore her gaze away, breaking whatever spell had captured her, and pushed past him. It took effort for her not to run. "If you intend to help me, you can put that tub in the freezer case up front."

As he followed, she heard his boots on the tile floor behind her. She should have heard him in the ballroom yesterday and here in the workroom a few minutes ago. But, no, both times she had been so wrapped up in thoughts of him, she hadn't noticed his approach. Not good at all when she needed to stay in control any time she was near him.

She had lost control with him once, and look what had happened.

At the freezer case, he slid the tub into the empty

space. To her relief, he then walked back around to the front of the counter.

Through the plate glass of the front window, she saw a family walking up to the shop. Her heart tripped a beat, whether from anxiety or elation, she wasn't sure.

"You can't stay here," she hissed.

"Why not? It's a store."

"But we can't talk here. Or now." Behind him, the door opened. She waved to the Walcotts and their two kids. The family went to their favorite table near the front of the store, and she glanced up at Tyler again. "Please go," she murmured.

"You'll talk to me when you get off work."

He hadn't made it a question. "Yes," she said between clenched teeth.

"What time do you finish up?"

She could tell him a lie. Give him a later time. Or, if the shop stayed as quiet as it was at the moment, she could tell him the truth, then rush through closing and leave before he returned.

Anything to avoid the conversation she didn't want to have.

He must feel as uneasy as she did about their impending talk, or why wouldn't he just have blurted out the crucial question and been done with it?

As wonderful as all her options for evading him sounded, she knew she couldn't be that devious. She sighed and admitted, "I'll be done in a couple of hours." At least that would give her time to collect her thoughts and plan exactly what she would say.

"All right, then," he agreed.

Relieved, she sagged against the counter.

"I'll just stick around," he added.

"But… I'm working."

"We covered that. And I've got nowhere to go except back to the Hitching Post. No sense in my driving all the way out there just to turn around and come back. Give me a triple dip of that butter pecan."

When she hesitated, he shot a glance toward the front table, where the Walcotts were still deciding on their own order.

He faced her again and leaned across the counter, bending down so close she could feel his breath against her cheek as he spoke quietly into her ear. "The Garlands corralled you at the Hitching Post yesterday. Then you ran off from the banquet room and never came back. And now, thanks to your customers, you've been saved by the bell. In case you weren't counting, that's three strikes for me. Do you seriously think I'm going to walk off and let you make yet another escape?"

Chapter Five

Three scoops of ice cream might have been more than he'd needed, but after witnessing Shay's obvious desire to see him gone, Tyler had been doubly determined to find an excuse to stick around.

He'd given her his exact reasons for his plan to stay. The question he'd thrown at her about her potential for an escape hadn't been idle talk, either. If he'd left the Big Dipper and come back again, he wouldn't have been a bit surprised to find the door locked and Shay long gone.

From the booth he'd taken in one corner of the room, he could watch her as she worked behind the counter. He could also listen as she chatted with one customer after another while filling their orders. Now, she had gone to the back room for something, and it was all he could do not to get to his feet and follow her.

The shop had stayed busy for the better part of an hour. It was as if everyone in Cowboy Creek was scheming to keep him from having things out with her.

Of course, that was paranoia talking.

Even as he had the thought, danged if the bell over the door didn't ring yet again. This time, he recognized the customer who entered. The man took one look at him, grinned, and headed in his direction.

Cole Slater slid into the seat opposite, and Tyler's heart slid down to the vicinity of his knees. Was he never going to get to talk to Shay alone?

Happy as he was to see his buddy, this wasn't the time or place he'd have chosen for them to get together.

Cole had no inkling of that, though. Still grinning, he reached for Tyler's hand. They shook, and the other man said, "Tina told me you were here."

"How did she know?" Tyler frowned in confusion.

"No, not *here* at the Dipper. I meant, in Cowboy Creek. We talked earlier today, but she was tied up getting ready for the wedding reception at the Hitching Post, and we didn't have time to get into much detail."

"Then what brings you to the Big Dipper?"

"Ice cream, what else? Hey, Shay!"

She had returned from the back room and looked over at their booth. Reluctantly, it seemed to Tyler, she headed their way. "A pint of the usual?" she asked Cole.

"You've got it. I'm surprising Tina. She gets cravings," he said to Tyler, then turned back to Shay. "How about you? Working right here in an ice cream shop, you ought to be able to get your fill of any flavor you like."

She shook her head. "No, I see it so much every day, ice cream's not on my list."

Tyler wondered what she *did* crave, but she didn't say.

"Let me know when you're ready and I'll get your order together." She walked away to greet an elderly pair who had come in and taken seats near the counter. As she stood beside their table, chatting, her hand went to her lower back.

Tyler frowned. With the weight she was carrying up front, she probably ought to be sitting once in a while, taking a break. Taking it easy.

"She's due even before Tina," Cole said, as if he'd watched Tyler watching Shay.

He nodded, but didn't comment. Right now, he didn't want to talk about due dates with anyone but Shay.

He sure couldn't escape the irony of this situation. All his life, his parents had nagged him about making something of himself. About acting like a responsible adult. Maybe they'd been right. Because, even unconfirmed, his suspicions regarding Shay had sent him on the run out at the ranch this afternoon.

Only the knowledge that he had to find out the truth had kept him from leaving Cowboy Creek altogether and brought him here tonight.

Deliberately, he changed the subject. "How's it feel to be on the verge of becoming a daddy again?" he asked Cole.

"Great. I highly recommend it. You ought to give it a try sometime."

He blinked. Could there be a chance he had jumped to the wrong conclusion about Shay's pregnancy? Was he going to make a fool of himself with his question to her?

"Are you planning to stick around for a while?" Cole asked. "Tina didn't say."

"That's because I haven't decided yet."

"Well, we'll have to make sure you stay longer than you did last time. I barely got to see you."

Last summer after meeting Shay, Tyler had spent most of his free time during the short visit hanging around the Big Dipper. Guilt made him cringe—until he recalled the circumstances. His buddy couldn't have had a clue about anything he'd gotten up to. "Not my fault, man. You took off on your honeymoon, remember?"

"That's not something I'll ever forget. But that's exactly my point."

"I don't plan to stay very long," he said truthfully.

Cole nodded. Normally, he could talk the ears off a donkey. But to Tyler's surprise, the other man stood abruptly, ready to depart. "We'll catch up when you get out to the ranch. Time for me to go home to my family."

He said those last two words with unmistakable pride. Pride and family—a combination Tyler didn't know much about.

Cole went to the counter to get his order, then waved farewell as he left the shop. Most of the other customers soon followed him, except the older couple near the counter.

When they finally made their slow way across the room, Tyler was about at the end of his patience. Shay seemed to miss that fact completely. After walking the pair to the door and waving goodbye, she turned the open sign to closed. She wiped down the couple's table and tucked their chairs neatly beneath it. She closed out the register and straightened up the counter. Then she disappeared into the back room and didn't return.

It felt too much like yesterday afternoon when she'd run off from the Hitching Post. He wouldn't put it past her to have slipped out a back door.

Frowning, he tossed his ice cream dish into a nearby trash container and stalked across the tile floor to the doorway behind the counter.

In the workroom, Shay stood with her back to him, leaning over an industrial-size dishwasher while she loaded ice cream scoops and metal milk shake containers into the compartment inside. As he watched, she paused to rest her hand against the washer's door. With her free hand, she rubbed her lower back. He felt another momentary pang of concern.

"Come take a load off." At the sound of his voice, she shied like a startled rabbit. "Sorry. Didn't mean to scare you."

"But insults don't require an apology?"

"Who insulted you?"

"You did. Is that what you think about pregnant women—they're just carrying a load?"

He ground his teeth together. So much for his show of concern. "It was a turn of phrase."

"One that turned in the wrong direction."

"Jed said the same thing to me this afternoon, and I didn't take offense. Maybe you're being overly sensitive." Or maybe that sensitivity came along with pregnancy. Suddenly, he felt as if he were walking on eggshells in the middle of a henhouse—a helluva place to be. "Let me rephrase it, then. Come and take a seat. We might as well both be comfortable, because there's no way I'm leaving until we're done talking."

"What if I have nothing to say?"

He laughed without humor. "You've said plenty already, even if you haven't run off at the mouth. Leaving the Hitching Post yesterday was only the first of a long list of clues."

She raised her chin belligerently, but he stared her down, waiting her out. He'd stay here all night, if necessary.

As if she could read that thought in his expression, she finally sighed and closed the dishwasher door. She crossed the workroom warily, the way a horse accustomed to mistreatment approached someone she feared would deliver more of it. A pang of regret flowed through him. Only his need to hear the truth from her kept him standing there.

When she came nearer, the light scent of her perfume surrounded him, unsettled him, bringing back a time he didn't want to think about.

"Have a seat," he said as pleasantly as he could. He gestured to the booth where he'd been sitting. "I've kept it waiting for you."

She slipped onto the bench and tried to slide behind the tabletop. Her belly, nearly pressed against the table's edge, made her movements awkward. The sight made him swallow hard. He took the seat across from her and knocked back the cup of water she'd given him along with his triple dip of ice cream.

She folded her hands on the tabletop in front of her.

Suddenly, his palms began to sweat. He wiped them on his jeans, rested his hands on his thighs and waited. Let her make the first move.

"Well, obviously," she said at last, "you're not here just because you had a sudden desire for my company. Or for ice cream."

"And obviously, you've got something you don't want to tell me."

She looked away. The pale green shirt she wore rose and fell with her deep breath. Her reaction didn't come as a shock. He knew what it meant. No matter what he'd tried to tell himself, or what that brief uncertainty he'd felt a few minutes ago tried to tell him, he had known the truth the moment she'd turned pale in the Hitching Post's dining room.

She turned back to him, her green eyes glittering. "I'm sure you've already guessed. I got pregnant the night we slept together."

"And you didn't think to tell me?"

"Why would I?"

He stared at her, not trusting himself to speak.

After a moment, she lifted her chin again as if it bolstered her courage to attack. "How exactly was I supposed to tell you? You didn't leave a forwarding address. And you never got in touch with me. What was I supposed to do, tell the Garlands I needed to contact you about a little something you left behind?"

"There's nobody else?" Again her face drained of color, and he realized how she had taken what he'd said—because he'd phrased it like a fool. "I mean, is there anybody else in the picture now?"

"Why is that important?"

"It's not, I guess." Or was it? He needed to get his head together and focus on what *did* matter. "When are you due?"

"In about three weeks."

He eyed what he could see of her over the tabletop. "Are you sure? You look as though you're…ready right now."

"I feel ready right now. But my doctors say otherwise. At least, at the moment. But they also say anything could happen."

The words acted like a kick to his gut. "Is something wrong?"

"No. But first babies can come early—"

He rubbed his palms against his jeans again.

"—especially when there's more than one of them."

"More than—? Are you telling me you're having twins?"

"No. Triplets."

His jaw dropped. He clamped his teeth together and stared at her until he could find his voice again. "You're saying you're having *three* babies?"

"That's usually what triplets means."

His ears rang, the way they had that time he'd been tossed from the back of a bull and jarred his skull against the hard-packed dirt. *Three babies...?*

Just as he had that day, he shook his head, as if he could throw off the noise and the blurred vision and bring himself back to normal. But he doubted he'd ever return to normal again.

She had tightened her jaw and crossed her arms high over her belly. He didn't appreciate the defensive position or her suddenly narrowed eyes. He sure didn't like the panic running though his entire system. This time, when he tried to speak, he could only gulp a mouthful of air. Cold sweat dotted his forehead. His fingers trembled so badly, he had to mimic her body language and tuck his hands under his arms.

How in hell was he going to deal with this?

Shay took one look at the terror in Tyler's eyes and, despite her anger at him, couldn't keep from feeling a rush of sympathy.

Seeing the results of the home pregnancy test had shocked her, too, but as she had already missed her period, she had suspected the indicator would turn blue. Dr. Grayden's announcement of the multiple babies had stunned her, but at least by then she had known for certain she was expecting.

For Tyler, all this had come…well…out of the blue.

Still, considering both how he had treated her and what she planned to say to him, she couldn't let sympathy get in the way. She tightened her arms across her chest and forced herself to keep her expression neutral. "Don't worry," she said evenly, "you're off the hook."

He looked even more shell-shocked. "Off the hook for what?"

Did he look relieved? She said nothing, letting a beat of silence go by.

"Are you telling me I'm not the dad, after all?"

The hope in his expression crushed her. In the two days she had agonized over informing him about her pregnancy, she had envisioned him happy at hearing she wasn't holding him responsible, ecstatic once he'd realized he wouldn't owe her anything. Somehow she hadn't realized she had still held on to the tiniest hope, too, that he would be glad to hear he was becoming a daddy.

"No," she said flatly. "I'm not telling you that. I'm just saying, as far as I'm concerned, that night with you never happened."

To her surprise, he gave a strangled laugh. "Kind of hard to get away with that story, isn't it, when no one can miss the obvious?"

"It's not so obvious. At least, not that you…were the one who got me pregnant. People will speculate all they want, and I can't stop them. But unless I make an announcement, nobody can know for sure who fathered my babies. *I* certainly don't intend to breathe a word. And I don't want you stepping up and acknowledging the fact it was you."

"Wait a minute…let me get this straight. You're saying you don't want anything from me?"

"Exactly."

His forehead creased in a frown. The skin around his eyes tightened. His mouth settled into a hard line. These were all responses she had never in a million years expected to see.

"And you're not planning to tell people?" he asked.

"No." It wasn't a lie. Other than Layne, who already knew, she didn't plan to discuss Tyler with anyone.

"That's not right."

In the pit of her stomach, she felt a butterfly flicker of fear. "It's not up to you who I tell and who I don't."

"Fine. Do what you want with that. But I'm not walking away without taking some responsibility for the situation."

Eight months of anger and resentment at him bubbled up inside her and overflowed. "We're not talking about a *situation*. They're three lives, three babies. They might not have been conceived in love—" Her voice cracked. She stopped, swallowed hard, went on. "But they're loved now. They'll come into this world knowing they're loved by me, and that's enough. They'll have me and my grandmother and our friends and each other, and none of us—especially me—needs you tagging along for the ride."

He reared back against his seat as if she'd slapped him. Sympathy flared inside her again but was quickly doused by another wave of the anger she had been forced to hide for so long. Getting carried away by these feelings couldn't be good for the babies. She took another deep breath, willing her temper and blood pressure to subside.

"You can forget trying to cut me out," he snapped. "I

don't walk away from my obligations, no matter what anyone thinks."

"I don't think anything. I'm just telling you how it's going to be—"

"And I'm telling you I won't—"

"Shay!"

At the sound of a woman shouting her name, Shay froze. So did Tyler. They had both leaned forward across the tabletop to stare each other down. Now they turned abruptly in the direction of the shout.

The clerk from the convenience store adjacent to the Big Dipper stood by the door in the far corner of the room, her hands fisted by her sides. "Are you all right? What's going on? Do you need me to call the sheriff?"

"No, no—everything's all right. Sorry, Beth. We were just…arguing a point. And with no one else in the shop, I guess we got a little carried away."

The other woman looked unconvinced.

Quickly, Shay made introductions, being careful to add, "Tyler is friends with Cole Slater and the Garlands."

"Uh-huh." *And not a friend of yours*, Beth's tone seemed to say. "Are we still planning to head out together?"

"Of course." Hiding her sigh of relief at this chance to escape, Shay edged out of the booth. "I'm almost ready to leave. You, too?"

"Yes."

"And Tyler was just about to go." She glanced his way, daring him to disagree. He had returned to leaning back against the booth, but he slid from his seat, then rose to tower over her.

"I'll leave through the store with Beth," she told him.

"You can go out the front door." She crossed the room ahead of him, attempting to seem relaxed but feeling acutely conscious of her awkward gait, Beth's wary expression, and the lingering anger she had seen in Tyler's dark blue eyes.

She held open the door. Without uttering a word, he resettled his Stetson.

"I'll say good-night here, then," she told him brightly, hoping her tone would convince Beth this was simply the end of a casual chat.

After a long moment of silence, he muttered, "I'll say this conversation is to be continued."

Chapter Six

A short while later, in the small house she shared with her grandmother, Shay collapsed onto the couch. Her confrontation with Tyler had left her body trembling with rage and her head swirling with emotions she didn't want to name. It was only when she was half-way home that she had finally stopped shaking.

She struggled to raise one tired leg and then the other, stretching them out on the couch cushion.

"Relax while you can, lass. The time will soon be here when you won't have a moment to yourself."

Shay smiled. Grandma Mo, as almost everyone in Cowboy Creek called her, had never lost the Irish lilt she'd picked up from her own parents and grandparents. The added flavor to her voice somehow made everything she said sound special to Shay.

"Can I get you something to eat?" Grandma asked now.

"No, thanks. I had some of the leftovers I took along with me tonight."

"That's good." As far back as Shay could remember, Grandma had had the full head of snow-white hair that somehow fit with her unlined peaches-and-cream complexion. She had the same green eyes she had passed down to her son and then to Shay. Those eyes twinkled as she glanced at Shay's stomach. "You don't want to go hungry. You're eating for a family now."

Though she had never named her babies' father, from the moment Shay had revealed she was pregnant, Grandma had stood by her, no questions asked. She had sat by her, too, in her rocking chair just a few feet from the couch. Over the winter months, while Shay's need to rest her feet grew at about the same rate as her middle, Grandma had knitted sweater after sweater, bootie after bootie, blanket after blanket, all meant for the impending arrival of her great-grandbabies. Shay's heart swelled every time she looked at the neat stacks already filling a shelf in her bedroom closet.

"Was the shop busy tonight?" Mo asked.

"Yes, especially in the first few hours. The Walcotts were in with both kids. And the Shaeffers stopped by, too."

"Del surely wasn't eating ice cream, with his sugar levels?"

There was no hiding anything in this town. "Sugar-free frozen yogurt," Shay reported.

"Good. I hope you didn't overdo it tonight. You look worn out."

"I'm tired," she admitted.

"That must be so. You're home early. Wasn't Layne in?"

When she and Layne worked the same nights, Shay would stop by SugarPie's to see her friend and stay for a cup of tea and a snack. Sometimes Beth came along and, afterward, Shay would often drop Beth at her apartment before heading home herself.

Tonight, the atmosphere in Shay's old car had felt

heavy with questions Beth wasn't asking and Shay didn't want to answer. When the other woman had yawned and said she was ready for an early night, Shay had nearly sighed in relief.

"Layne was in," she said. "But Beth and I decided to skip SugarPie's tonight."

"Sugar mentioned you hadn't been by."

Shay shot her grandmother a look. Grandma sat focusing on the bootie she was currently knitting—which was a dead giveaway that she was attempting to appear innocent. Mo could knit an entire wardrobe almost without looking at her needles.

Shay laughed. "I guess the gossip mill wasn't a bit tired this evening, was it?"

Along with Jed Garland, Grandma and Sugar were the biggest storehouses of gossip in Cowboy Creek. And Shay didn't doubt there was plenty of that floating around concerning her pregnancy. But really, with Tyler gone from town so soon after she had met him, folks couldn't have any definite knowledge that he was her babies' father. As she had told him, they might wonder, but they couldn't *know*.

Suddenly she sobered. Word about Tyler's return could easily have made it into town by now. But neither Grandma nor Sugar could have learned about his visit to the Big Dipper tonight…could they?

The memory of his statement about continuing their conversation made her shudder. She pulled the afghan from the arm of the couch and wrapped it around her. If either of the women had any inkling she and Tyler had talked about her pregnancy, that she had told him he was the father of her children…

Another shiver ran through her.

Sugar and Grandma would gang up on her—out of concern for her and her babies, of course. Sugar had never had children and Grandma had lost her only son when he had gotten hooked on following the rodeo. Yet they both strongly believed a family should stay together. They would try to help fix things between her and Tyler.

But she and Tyler never would be a family. And what was wrong between them could never be fixed.

AFTER BEING THROWN out of the Big Dipper, Tyler had tossed and turned for most of the night, wasting valuable sleep time in his comfortable bed at the Hitching Post. He had risen early, dressed and gone straight to saddle up Freedom. It being Sunday and too early for the hotel guests even to have had breakfast, the corral was deserted.

From a distance, he saw Jed's ranch manager headed toward the barn, but he simply waved at the man and turned Freedom toward the trail beyond the corral.

The morning air was cool enough for him to want a jacket, but not cold enough to help clear his head.

As it turned out, his path and Cole's had never crossed again last night, and by the time he returned to the barn, he was glad to find his buddy inside. Cole stood at a workbench where he was cleaning tack, a job that could never be set aside on a working ranch.

When Freedom was back in his stall, Tyler grabbed a bucket of water and joined Cole.

"You looking for work?" Cole asked. Unlike at their meeting at the Big Dipper, this morning he seemed more than ready to talk. "If you're job hunting, I hate to tell you, but Pete's gone back to his house already, and Jed hasn't been out yet to make his morning rounds. Don't bother trying to impress me. I'm just one of the hired hands."

"And Jed's first new grandson-in-law."

Cole snorted. "First in a line, which also doesn't impress anybody. And if he comes after you, don't say I didn't warn you. Don't get me wrong, Jed's happy for the additions to the family and more than pleased about the baby Tina and I have on the way. He's all about adding to his list of great-grandkids. But I really might've won a special place in his heart if I'd managed to get his granddaughter pregnant with a few of those kids at once."

Down on one knee, Tyler froze with his hand clenched around the sponge. Cole knew. How could he not, considering the crack he'd just made?

So much for believing what Shay had said last night. *I certainly don't intend to breathe a word.*

His stomach churned in a slow boil. His face grew hot from discomfort and anger. Did she really think she could get away with her lie? That no one would say anything to him before he left town?

He stood and met Cole's eyes. "Who told you?"

"Tina."

"You could have said something, man."

"I didn't hear about it until I got home last night. I don't think anybody knew for sure until they saw you and Shay together again. And even I'm not supposed to know everything."

"What's that mean? Shay swore the whole damned town to secrecy so I wouldn't find out?"

"Whoa." Cole dropped his sponge into the bucket

beside him. Arms crossed, he stared. "You're saying this is a surprise to you?"

"Damn right it is. All of it. Including the fact Shay's carrying more than one baby."

Cole gave a long, low whistle. "That's what you get for not returning my calls for the past few months. I'd hassle you more about that, except it looks like you've got enough to deal with at the moment. Anyhow, my point is, if you had replied to my messages—or come by for Christmas, like I asked—you and I might have figured it out sooner. I had my suspicions about you two once Shay started showing, but Tina finally confirmed my thoughts last night."

"You didn't know before then?"

"Nope. Scout's honor. I wasn't about to bring up your name around here until we talked. I imagine Jed and Paz and the rest of the women suspected the truth from the beginning, but they didn't let me in on the news. The Garland family can play their hands close to the vest when they want to." He shook his head and whistled again. "I'm getting nervy over one baby on the way, and you're having three at once."

"Don't remind me."

"Somebody has to. Those kids are going to be here before you can turn around."

"What did you mean, that you're not supposed to know everything?"

For the first time, Cole hesitated. Then he shrugged. "What the heck. Friends have to stick together—even if they don't always return phone calls. The thing is, you already know Jed decided to try a little matchmaking when he brought me and Tina together. He hasn't let up since, not with any of his granddaughters or even my sister, Layne. Nobody's said anything definite to me, but I'm betting you're next on the list."

When he could catch his breath again, Tyler gave a hollow laugh. "Considering the way Shay and I left things last night, Jed won't have any chance of playing matchmaker. I doubt I'll be seeing her again."

"I wouldn't count on that one, buddy."

Tyler narrowed his eyes and said flatly, "What."

"She's coming out to the hotel this afternoon."

He'd forgotten Paz had said that yesterday. Maybe it was for the best. What had sounded then like a long time away now seemed much too soon. But like it or not, he would have to see Shay. He would have to get a few things straightened out with her. Finish their conversation, the way he'd promised her last night.

A heavy lump dragged him down, the same weight he'd felt since the moment she had made her announcement about the babies—the weight of responsibilities he hadn't expected or intended to have.

Life with his folks had cured him of the idea of ever getting married or raising a family. With his parents as role models, he wouldn't know the first thing about raising a kid. But now he was facing becoming the father of not one, not two, but three babies—in only a few weeks!

He could imagine his father's scorn at hearing he'd been irresponsible enough to sleep with Shay without using protection. That was the least of his worries now. He had to do the right thing for these kids, financially, at least, both to prove to his parents he was a responsible man and for his own peace of mind.

Of course, the *real* right thing was to be a *real* daddy. He wasn't going there. He wasn't cut out for the role.

And, as Shay had made sure to stress last night, he wasn't the man she'd choose for the job.

BY MIDAFTERNOON SUNDAY, Shay had changed her mind a half dozen times about whether or not to keep her appointment with Jed. At the moment, she wasn't up to talking to her boss or any of the Garlands—and most especially not to Tyler. If she hadn't so badly needed the extra income from her job at the Hitching Post, she would have canceled the meeting without a second thought.

Of course, the minute she drove into the parking area behind the hotel, the first person she saw was the one she didn't want to see. Tyler stood in the barn doorway with a couple of the ranch's cowhands. When he spied her car, he appeared to break off his conversation and strode in her direction.

She clutched the steering wheel for a moment, took a deep breath and let it out again. "Brace yourselves, babies," she said, looking down at her stomach. "This could get ugly."

As he approached, she considered simply rolling down the window and waiting. Let him bend down from his great height to talk with her. She could rest her back and legs. On the other hand, she would also be caught without a way to make her escape.

That thought had her out of the car and slamming the door shut before he could reach her.

He came to a halt in front of her. "I told you our conversation would be continued."

"Not for very long. Jed's waiting for me. But we might as well finish what we have to say right here and be done with it."

She exhaled heavily. She had practiced her part in this talk over and over in her mind all morning. She could say what she had to say now. For the sake of her babies. Yes, they needed a daddy, but not one who claimed that relationship simply by right of their birth. They needed someone who would love them and care about them as much as she already did.

"I let my temper get away from me when we talked last night," she admitted. "But I meant what I told you about being off the hook."

"What if I don't choose to be? Don't I have a say?"

"Why would you?"

"Because those kids you're carrying are mine, too."

His eyes glittered in the sunshine, more from repressed anger than concern, she was sure. Again, she had to remind herself of the responses she had rehearsed. "And are you planning to be their daddy? Planning to…to be a family with us?"

"Whoa." He raised his hands and backed up a step, as if she were a horse that had suddenly gone wild. "I never said either of those things. Neither one of them was ever in my plans."

"I thought not." Clearly, he had also never considered the word that wouldn't leave her lips, either. The *M* word. "Well, it doesn't matter. When it comes down to it, we barely know each other, do we? And we obviously seem to care about each other even less."

She waited a beat, but he said nothing, which only reinforced what she had feared all along. He had never cared about her. How could she believe he would feel anything for her babies?

Unable to look at him, she began walking toward the hotel.

She *had* cared about him, at least in those days he'd spent in Cowboy Creek. She had just lied about that.

When he fell into step beside her, she swallowed a bitter laugh, admitting she had also failed dismally at fooling herself. She knew many things about him. How he held a woman when he slow danced. How he liked to flirt. How he liked to kiss. How he went after what he wanted.

Right down to her bones, she had known he would follow her now, that he wouldn't give up. As if he planned to prevent her from getting away, he walked close beside her, close enough that she picked up the scents of his aftershave and his freshly washed cotton shirt. His boots were free of dust and scuff marks, as if he'd worn his Sunday best. For her?

The thought left her swallowing another laugh. Even she couldn't fool herself about that.

A quick glance around the stable yard and ahead toward the Hitching Post showed her they were alone. Once they went inside the hotel, they would lose any chance of a conversation without witnesses.

She stopped abruptly, then waited until he turned to face her. "They're not your children, Tyler. Not the way that's supposed to mean. I don't understand why you believe you even have the right to a say."

"They're my responsibility, that's why. At least until they're of legal age."

Her breath caught in her chest. Even knowing how little he cared, that dry, flat statement hit like a slap to her face. To her senses. "Just how do you think this parenting thing works? You support your children all through childhood, then dump them when they become adults?"

"By that age, they need to learn to accept responsibility for themselves."

"You brought up that word last night. You said they were your responsibility. Your *obligation*." She shook her head. "To you, they're a temporary investment, but to me, they're the children I'll love for the rest of my life. Don't you see the difference?"

Chapter Seven

Even as Shay asked the question, she knew in her heart Tyler wouldn't understand. How could he? He had already admitted to her he had never wanted to be a daddy or to have a family. And as much as it hurt to acknowledge it to herself, she had been right. All those months ago, he had only been looking for a good time, not a relationship that could lead to a lifetime commitment.

A few yards away from them, the door of the Hitching Post opened. Her boss stepped out onto the back porch, his face creased in a familiar smile, and her spirits lifted. Immediately, she lost her reluctance to meet with Jed. Now, she wanted only to thank him for the rescue.

"Looking for me?" she asked as cheerfully as she could. "Here I am." Carefully holding the wooden railing, she climbed the steps and, at Jed's sweeping gesture, let him usher her into the hotel.

She walked beside him down the long hallway to the Hitching Post's banquet room, her ears tuned to the sound of boots on the hardwood floor behind her. A sound that never came.

"What's your hurry, girl?" he asked. "Take it slow, or else you'll be giving those babies a bumpy ride."

Smiling for his benefit, she stroked her stomach and slowed her pace. She *had* been hurrying, for once not caring who noticed her ungainly stride. She had been trying to put more distance between herself and Tyler. And yet she couldn't help wondering why he hadn't followed them into the hotel.

"Bet you're curious about why I wanted to see you today," Jed said.

"I am, actually. Very curious." She envisioned crossing her fingers on both hands, hoping he had found some additional hours for her. From the ballroom up ahead, she heard a burst of laugher, which helped to reinforce her wish. "I guess Tina and the rest of the girls are working overtime this afternoon, too."

"You might say that." His blue eyes twinkling, he grinned at her and stopped short of the wide doorway. Again, he gallantly ushered her in ahead of him.

Immediately, the air was filled with the sounds of women clapping and yelling, *"Surprise!"*

Through a sudden blur, Shay looked around the crowded ballroom to see the face of almost every adult woman she knew in Cowboy Creek.

Jed gave her a hug. "I'll leave you and the ladies to it. Have fun!"

"Thanks." Quickly, she kissed his cheek.

Tina stood at the head of the room, waving to Shay from beside a comfortably padded lounge chair draped with ribbons. "It's all yours," she called.

"It's even got a footrest," Tina's best friend, Ally, added.

Shay laughed. "That sounds perfect." She stopped at a table to hug her grandmother and Sugar. "Grandma,

I can't believe you didn't breathe a word of this to me last night."

"And where would the surprise have been in that?" Grandma asked archly.

"Don't worry," Sugar said, "I kept her busy on the phone so she wouldn't have too much time to chat."

"And so I could fall asleep," Shay guessed.

"So the *babies* could fall asleep," Grandma said with a smile.

Shay continued to the front of the banquet hall. The room had been decorated with pale blue streamers and pink balloons. Pastel paper umbrellas dangled from the chandeliers. A long table off to one side of the room held a row of metal chafing dishes and a large pink-and-blue-frosted sheet cake. Another table was piled high with packages tied with pastel ribbons and adorned with baby rattles, booties and other small gifts.

"How did you manage all this so quickly after the reception in here?" she asked Tina as she settled herself in the lounger. Maybe today's surprise explained why Jed had told her she wasn't needed to work last night. They didn't want to risk her finding out about the shower.

Jed was very good at arranging people's lives. She recalled what Tyler had said about Jed's claim he would be busy at the reception. At the time, she had found that odd. Now she wondered if her boss had had a reason for deliberately leaving Tyler on his own last night. But he couldn't have suspected Tyler would track her down at the Big Dipper...could he?

"We had no trouble getting everything ready," Tina said. "Abuelo rounded up some willing helpers to give us a hand."

She couldn't keep from wondering if Tyler had been

one of those helpers and what he was up to at the moment. Then she pushed the thoughts aside. She wasn't going to let anything upset this special celebration for her babies.

Ally, her dark eyes wide and sparkling, came up to Shay and gestured toward her stomach. "*Chica*, you've gotten so big since the last time I saw you."

"I know," she said happily. "Stick around. My doctors have me counting kicks, and the babies have been active."

"We're not going to have to cut this party short, are we?" Tina asked, smiling.

Shay shook her head. "No, I think we're good. And one day, Ally, we'll be having a party like this for you."

"Oh, no, not me," the other woman said in pretend horror. She fluffed her long dark hair and added, "Thanks, anyway. But between you and Tina, we'll have enough babies around to last us for quite a while. That lets me off the hook."

At the echo of her own words to Tyler, Shay had to force herself to continue smiling.

Think about the babies.

Don't think about the man who fathered them or what he might be up to right now.

SUNDAY WAS A day of rest for the hands on Garland Ranch, except for those whose turn it was to work with the hotel guests.

For lack of anything else to keep him busy, Tyler had volunteered to help out this afternoon. With those guests now all saddled up and paired with a cowhand, he'd run out of things to do.

He fought the urge to run. Restlessly, he paced the corral fence line.

A dozen yards away, Jed stood with one elbow propped on the fence's top rail and his Stetson tilted back, and somehow Tyler knew the older man was waiting for him. He walked in that direction, feeling like a kid being called on the carpet once again—though only grass and bare earth lay underfoot, and Jed wasn't like his father.

Shaking off the crazy thoughts, he walked up to the ranch owner.

"You have a nice way with the guests," Jed said.

Not at all like his father. "Thanks," he said, smiling.

"'Specially the young ones."

The smile slid away.

"Cole said you and he talked earlier this afternoon."

"We did."

"Good. Then there's no need for me to beat around the bush about Shay and the babies, is there? What I want to know is, what do you intend to do?"

He might have felt taken aback by what seemed like outright hostility on Jed's part, except the man's gruffness couldn't hide the kindness in his face. Cole had long ago told him Jed had a heart of gold. He also knew Jed made a point of looking out for everyone in town. And then, of course, there was the man's sideline in matchmaking. If Cole had been right, Jed planned to turn his attention to *him*.

"I appreciate your interest," he said sincerely, "but first of all, you need to know that where I'm concerned, there's no sense wasting your time planning another wedding."

To his surprise, Jed nodded. "I agree. Son, the last

thing I'd want to do is ruin my winning streak. But that doesn't mean I want to see you shirking your responsibility."

There was that word again, the one Shay hadn't hesitated to throw back in his face. "Yeah, well, at least you and I are in agreement there." He leaned back against the fence and glared at the Hitching Post.

"Then what's the problem?"

"Try putting that idea across to the other party."

Now Jed chuckled. "That Shay's a stubborn one, just like her grandma Mo. But don't go telling anyone I said that."

"I won't, if you won't repeat any of this conversation."

"You've got my word on that." After a while, Jed added, "Mo and Shay have been on their own for quite some time. Along with the stubbornness they share, Mo gave that girl a big helping of independence."

"That's a good thing. But from now on, it's going to be more than just the two of them—with the babies coming along," he added in a hurry.

"And isn't that something," Jed said wonderingly. "First time Cowboy Creek has had a family with triplets. It's an amazing thought. It was a bit of a shock for you, I'd imagine."

"That's an understatement. And as you said, it's a responsibility. One I don't intend to walk away from."

"Good." Jed clapped him on the shoulder. "I have to say, I'm proud of you for wanting to man up and do the right thing."

For a moment, he couldn't respond. After knowing him less than a year, Jed had given him a compliment his own father never had. "Thanks," he said, now sounding gruff himself. For a minute, he watched the horses in the corral patiently carrying the weight of people on their backs and walking in circles. He could relate. "Guess I'll head over to my room to clean up."

"And after that," Jed said, "here's what I'd recommend. You need to track Shay down and see if you can't come to some kind of understanding. After all, it's for the good of those babies. For their sakes, there has to be a way you two can set aside your differences."

Don't you see the difference? Shay had asked.

Maybe he couldn't, not the way she had put things. But that couldn't keep him from fulfilling his obligations.

THE CAKE HAD been cut and devoured by the attendees at the shower. One by one, the women had given Shay hugs and goodbyes before leaving the ballroom. Layne had gone into town for her shift at SugarPie's, and Ally had left, too.

Grandma and Sugar had stood at the doorway seeing everyone off. Now they, along with Jane, had disappeared. They had probably gone to the kitchen to help Paz and the waitresses with the leftovers—not that there were many of those. She wondered whether the men in the Garland family would get their share. Jed's grandsons-in-law…and Tyler.

With so many people constantly around her this afternoon, she had hoped she could stop thinking about him. Instead, with every package she opened, she was reminded of the dreams she had so briefly built around him in the few days after they had met. Dreams she no longer believed in.

She and Tina sat alone at the head table, both of them with their feet up on chairs.

The gifts had all been opened, and every time she looked across to the table at one side of the ballroom, her eyes filled with tears.

"You've got a lot of presents to take with you," Tina said with a smile.

"I sure do." Each gift she'd received had been matched twice over. "Three playpens. A trio of car seats. And every outfit and accessory a baby could need, in triplicate. I don't know how I'll ever thank everyone for being so generous."

"Your reaction today was thanks enough. They're all thrilled to know they're helping to make you and the babies happy."

"They've done that, all right." She felt tears welling again. "And thanks to Grandma, I've already got three cribs at home. But I don't know how I'm going to fit all this into the babies' bedroom."

"That's the good thing about infants. Everything they own is in miniature. Of course, they don't stay that way for long."

"Please, let's not go there. I don't want to look that far ahead. The thought of taking care of three infants, let alone dealing with three toddlers, is already enough to overwhelm me."

"Don't worry. You'll be surprised at how quickly you adapt."

"I hope so."

Grandma and Sugar reappeared in the ballroom and approached their table.

"How's the cake?" Sugar asked.

Shay took another tiny forkful from the plate in front

of her, swallowed it and rolled her eyes. "Phenomenal, as usual. But I'm afraid to dig in or I'll break the scale at my doctor's appointment tomorrow." Now that she was so close to her delivery date, she was seeing either Dr. Grayden or the specialist in Santa Fe twice weekly. "I've decided I'll have one good-size mouthful of cake for each baby."

"And one for yourself, as well," Grandma said.

Shay rolled her eyes again. "If you don't stop," she pretended to scold, "you'll have me as big as a house by the time your great-grands come along."

"As long as they're healthy, lass, that's all that matters."

"We've just talked to Jed," Sugar said. "He's going to get some of the boys to help you load your car."

"That's great." Shay put her feet on the floor and prepared to stand.

The sound of boot steps in the hall and then the appearance of a handful of men in the doorway made her settle back into her seat.

Jed led the way into the room.

Behind him followed both Tina's and Jane's husbands...and Tyler. Even seeing him from this distance made her heart skip a beat. He was the tallest of the three younger men and, no doubt about it in her opinion, the hottest looking. He had changed into a pale green shirt that contrasted with his dark hair. Up close, it would make his eyes look an even deeper blue. Deep enough to drown in, as the saying went.

But now, at least, she had more sense than that.

"Looks like you could use a trailer for all your loot," Jed said.

"I'm sure we can manage to fit it into my car," she told him.

"Not of all it. You'll need another vehicle."

She had a sinking feeling she knew where this conversation was going. Tyler was the only unattached male in the room, aside from Jed. And Jed would never pass up a chance to fulfill his role as Cowboy Creek's head matchmaker. "That's fine," she said hurriedly. "Grandma can—"

"I left my car in town," Grandma broke in. "Sugar drove, and she has to get back to the shop. We're just leaving."

"Oh. Well." She tried again. "Jed, please don't have anyone go to any trouble. I can take some of the gifts home today and then pick up the rest tomorrow."

"Why do that when I've got an able-bodied assistant right here?" He clapped Tyler on the shoulder. "Son, you wouldn't mind helping Shay get all her gifts to her house, would you?"

"No, not at all."

She swallowed a groan of pure frustration.

Tina led the younger men over to the side table.

Jed remained standing beside Mo and Sugar.

After one glance at their smiling faces, she knew there was no point in arguing. They were determined to have this happen. They had probably conspired to *make* this happen.

Like it or not—and she didn't—she would have to accept Tyler's help.

Chapter Eight

As Shay entered through the front door, it was impossible for her not to know Tyler had come into the house directly behind her. The sound of his heels rapping against the oak flooring nearly drowned out her lighter steps.

She switched on a table lamp near the doorway. The soft light accentuated the wooden accents of the couch and chairs and burnished the maple of Grandma's rocker. The light played up the jewel tones of the afghan she had left in a heap on the cushions that afternoon. To her the lived-in room had always represented an equal measure of security and love. She hoped it would mean the same to all three of her babies.

Tyler carried two armloads of packages while she, at his insistence, held only the handles of a shopping bag filled with boxes of baby clothes. Truthfully, she admitted to herself that even adding that small amount of weight on one side left her more unsteady than ever. So did being near Tyler again.

For such a brief time, she had had so many dreams about him, so many hopes. Now she had only the need to keep him from ever knowing how hard she had fallen.

"I could have carried another bag," she said. "It

would have evened out my load. Besides, I told you it was just a short walk to the front door."

"You didn't need to tell me. I've been here before."

"I haven't forgotten," she snapped. Too late, she realized it was probably the wrong thing to say. He didn't need to know that night still lingered in her memory. Grimly, she held on to her anger and irritation, knowing they would keep her safe from so many other emotions she couldn't afford to feel. "Well, it was easier for me to agree to carry a lighter load than to stand there arguing with you."

"And the faster we unload the car, the sooner I can leave, right?"

He wasn't asking. He had mocked her tone, telling her he knew what she was thinking. She pretended to misunderstand. "You know," she said as pleasantly as she could manage, "no one's forcing you to do this. You can leave everything down here in the living room. There's nowhere to put the gifts in the bedroom, anyhow, except in piles on the floor."

"That's good enough. They'll be near at hand for when you need them."

Swallowing a groan, she crossed the room but came to a stop at the foot of the stairs. She might as well have stood looking up at a mountain soaring above her. Already short of breath after the brief walk from the car to the house, she would have no chance of quickly leading the way up to the second floor.

"You go ahead. I'll only slow you down. I switched rooms a few months ago, so the babies could have my bigger bedroom." Her face flamed from a mixture of awkwardness at the reference to their past and her irritation now. She gestured to the staircase. "Second door on the left. You probably remember the way."

"Yeah."

He moved swiftly up the stairs. She followed much more slowly. Her head filled with images of what had happened between them the last time—the one and only time—he had been here, images she didn't want to remember but couldn't make herself forget.

Suddenly, she felt overwhelmed at having him in the house with her again. Physically, he took up too much space, upsetting the comfort she normally felt here. His presence brought back too many memories, too many emotions, and she was hit with the realization of why she had brought him home with her in the first place. She hadn't made the decision based on just how well they got along, how easily he made her laugh, how close she felt to him after only a few days.

She had brought him home because she had fallen in love with him the night she met him.

And he had fallen far short of the man she'd thought he was.

Before she reached the landing, he returned and started down again. While she wouldn't change her current physical state for anything in the world, she wished she could recall the last time she'd had that much energy.

Keep it light. Keep him from knowing how much you care.

"Show-off," she muttered.

With a laugh, he stopped beside her. "I'd be slow, too, if I were carrying that much weight."

"Gee, thanks. You're really good with an insult."

"You know what I mean." He touched her arm. "Hey, you okay? You look all in."

"I'm all right." Or she *would* be, if only he would never again touch her or look at her the way he was looking at her now.

He stood a couple of steps below her, which put them on a level. On this side of the living room where the lamplight couldn't penetrate the shadows, his eyes appeared darker than ever, blue-black and gleaming and filled with something she didn't want to think of as concern.

"I'm fine," she said firmly. "It's just been a long day." A longer weekend. An even longer eight months.

"Why don't you sit and let me take care of everything."

Oh, no. She wouldn't fall for that line, no matter how good it sounded. He would be gone soon, and good riddance, and she would be on her own again. "You're letting Jed's compliments go to your head. You might be able-bodied, especially compared to me right now, but that doesn't mean I'm helpless."

"I never thought you were. And I wouldn't let Jed's words concern you. He was only being nice so I'd go along with him."

"Now, why does that seem familiar, cowboy?"

He frowned. "That's hitting below my champion belt buckle, Shay."

She couldn't keep from glancing at that buckle.

"Impressive, huh?"

She snapped her gaze up and found him grinning at her. "Not at all. It's just a reminder you're only a rodeo cowboy, which still doesn't impress me. And I don't make things up, I just call them as I see them."

"So do I. That night at Cole's wedding, I saw a woman who was as ready to flirt with me as I was to flirt with her." She refused to react or even to look at him, but he touched her chin, bringing her gaze to his again. He leaned closer and said quietly, "I saw a woman who wanted me as much I wanted her. How do you call that one, Shay? Are you planning to deny it?"

She couldn't speak, let alone deny his words. Arguing would only make her a liar. For the first time in her life, she had let herself get close to a cowboy. And she *had* wanted him, almost from the minute she had met him. Only she had been thinking about forever and he had wanted a one-night stand.

Even now, she longed to lean closer—an irrational thought but one she struggled to control. His hand on her chin and his face so close to hers revived the most special memories she had ever known.

As if he'd read her mind, he said, "We had a good time, Shay. And when it comes to what happened as a result, I'm willing to take some of the blame. But not all of it." He dropped his hand. "For the record, when I said you should sit and let me take care of things, I wasn't attempting to get anything out of you, just giving you a chance to rest. Don't judge me by what happened in the past. We're in the here and now, and I'm trying to do what's right." He moved past her and continued down the stairs.

As the front door closed behind him, she patted her stomach with an unsteady hand. "Don't worry, babies, I'm not falling for any of that. He's just trying to make himself look good. Your da—"

Oh, no. She also wasn't falling into that trap.

"Your *mommy's* the one in charge around here, and she's perfectly capable of taking care of you all by herself."

She didn't need the help of a rodeo cowboy.

Thanks to her father, she knew all about the lies they told, the promises they broke, the important events they didn't attend, the holidays they missed. She would be doing her babies a favor by keeping Tyler out of their lives.

THREE DAYS LATER, Tyler sat in his truck outside Shay's house. He tried not to think about what had happened inside that small two-story building on his last visit, and especially not what had happened when he'd gone upstairs with her the previous summer.

After bringing her home with the bounty from her baby shower, he had spent the next couple of days seething over her insults—which, unlike his unfortunate turns of phrase, were very much intended. First, her hint that he'd said things to her just to get what he wanted, and then her odd emphasis when she'd called him *only* a rodeo cowboy. Both had been designed to hit him right where it hurt.

He glanced down the empty street. Jed had assured him Shay would be there within the hour. Tyler had no doubt the old man was up to something.

These past few days, Jed had gotten him to spend plenty of time helping his granddaughters around the hotel. Their grandpa also had taken every opportunity to make sure his new assistant wasn't far from Shay whenever she came to work at the Hitching Post.

He could see right through the older man's scheme. Jed had accepted his statement about not being interested in matchmaking services. In fact, he had seemed relieved at not having to risk his perfect record. Still, he appeared to want to help pave the way to a truce.

Tyler didn't have the heart to tell the man again he was wasting his time and talents.

From the other end of the block, a car approached. He recognized the sedan's outlines, then the dust covering every inch of the vehicle and, finally, the silhouette of the woman inside. He braced himself for the unhappy reception he expected. He didn't have long to wait.

Before she'd even put the car into Park, he could see Shay's frown. She had been brief and formal when she'd thanked him for his help the other day. At the Hitching Post in the presence of others, she had been civil enough. Now, evidently, it was a case of her rodeo, her rules. He slammed the door of his truck and went to meet her at the walkway to the house.

Her face looked drawn and tired. Her gaze seemed unfocused with fatigue. He clenched his fist by his side to keep from reaching up and smoothing away the lines in her forehead. It was almost a welcome relief to see a fire suddenly light her eyes.

"What are you doing here?" she demanded.

"I've come to help you set up the baby's room."

"Jed told me he would have Cole do that, which is why I hurried home from the shop. What happened to him?"

"He's still out riding the ranch."

"And Pete?"

"Waiting for the vet to take a look at one of the foals."

"And Mitch?"

He held back a growl. Barely. "I imagine the deputy sheriff's busy keeping your fair town safe from evildoers. And before you ask, the rest of the cowhands are taking care of their chores and the stable boy's mucking out the stalls and Jed's too old to be moving furniture—but don't tell him I said that. So the deal is, you're stuck with me."

"Thanks, but I'll pass."

"And not have the room put to rights before the kids come along?"

Her face settled into the determined scowl of a bull protecting his territory. Likewise, he felt himself stiffening, preparing to dig in his heels. Whether or not Jed had misguidedly instigated this arrangement on his behalf, he had agreed to help, and that's just what he intended to do.

And, unlike last time he'd come here, he also intended to keep his hands off Shay.

"Look," he said patiently, "once I left town last summer, I couldn't have known you'd gotten pregnant, but I know it now. You don't want me to have a role in the kids' lives. I get that, and I told you I don't want to be a daddy, anyway. But I'm leaving in a few days. I want to make sure you're all set up before the babies come. And then after I'm gone, I'll send you money every month to help take care of them. It's the least I can do."

Now her expression changed to disbelief and distrust. The sight hit him harder than the verbal insults she'd thrown at him.

Who would have won the standoff, he didn't know. As it turned out, events didn't have time to come to a head.

The front door of the house opened, and Shay's grandma stepped onto the porch. She was carrying a handbag and a couple of plastic sacks. As she came down the steps, she left the door open behind her. Tyler had met the woman at the Hitching Post, though they hadn't yet had a private conversation. Maureen, her name was. She had told him to call her Mo.

He didn't know if she knew he was the father of Shay's babies, and she'd never given him an indication one way or the other. But she had both a head of white hair and a sharp eye in common with Jed, and the two older folks appeared to have a shared interest in helping Tyler's cause.

"Ah, Tyler," she said with satisfaction. "Jed told me you'd be here shortly. I'm glad you've made it and Shay is home now, too. I have to run, and it wouldn't have been much of a welcome to leave you sitting out on the porch."

He hadn't received much of a welcome, anyhow. "It wouldn't be a hardship to spend some time in that porch swing up there," he countered, a pleasure he and Shay had never shared.

"Well," Mo said with a smile, "maybe you'll have that opportunity after your work is done today."

The look Shay shot him told him he'd have no chance of that. Her expression softened as she turned to Mo. "Don't you want to stay and help us set up the room?"

"I would love to, lass, but I'm on my way to the community center."

"I'm sure they could manage without you for once."

"Not this time." Mo gestured to her sacks. "I've got the rest of the yarn for our current project, and the knitting circle can't make progress without it. No, you two go along and get to work. I'll be up to see the room as soon as I'm back again."

She stepped aside on the walkway, giving them space to pass her, and stood there smiling. And waiting.

He could see Shay struggling, unwilling to give in and accept his help. Maybe what he had said about not having the room ready in time finally swayed her, because after another beat of silence, she nodded. "All right, see you later."

As Shay started up the walkway toward the house, Mo patted his arm encouragingly.

This time when the urge to smile struck him, he didn't fight it. He'd have to save his battle strength for when he and Shay were alone.

AFTER TYLER FOLLOWED Shay upstairs to the bedroom that used to be hers, she quickly ran down a list of what needed to be done. Of course she wouldn't want him spending any more time here with her than he absolutely had to. As she probably had it figured, the sooner she outlined what he had to take care of, the sooner he could get to it and be on his way.

"The cribs still need to be assembled, and when that's finished, we can set them up with the changing table and bureaus. And then I can fill the drawers." She gestured across the room. "You can see I didn't make much progress with the bags from the shower," she mumbled.

He'd wager she wouldn't confess to what he knew had to be the reason, that she was more worn out than she let on.

As he worked on unboxing the first crib, she moved around the room, unpacking bags and going back and forth to put things in the closet. When he started his assembly, she was at his side, helping to steady the railing as he lined up the head- and footboards and slipped the bolts into place.

He frowned. "Shouldn't you be taking it easier?"

"I'm just holding on to a strip of wood."

"You're on your feet. And you've been on your feet a good part of the day. Don't you want to sit down?"

"Don't you want to get this done?"

He tightened one of the bolts. "I'm not in that much of a hurry."

"Well, I am."

With one hand, she stroked her round belly, a move he'd seen her make many times at the Hitching Post. Now, he saw her belly move in response. He stared as the stripes on her shirt rippled like a windblown wheat field. His heart thumped and his throat tightened and for the first time the truth of what she had said to him the other day hit home. These were three babies she was carrying, three lives she would soon bring into the world.

"The babies are active today," she said, looking down, a soft smile curving her lips.

Once, she had shared those smiles with him. Those days were gone. The thought left him feeling hollow.

"Guess the kids are getting ready to come take up residence in these cribs." Suddenly, he felt less irritated about her need to hurry him along. Maybe it wasn't directed solely at her desire to get him out of her house. Maybe she knew more than she was telling him. His hand slipped. The tool that had come with the kit nicked a tiny scratch into the wood of the headboard. "You've still got a couple more weeks left, at least, right?"

She laughed without humor. "Are you worried I might go into labor as we speak?"

"Heck, no," he fibbed. "Just thinking about how long it might take me to set up three cribs. It's not as easy as just one." He paused, then said, "Raising three babies at once can't be as easy as just one, either."

"I don't know about that. You just batch tasks and get everything over with at once." The twitch at one corner of her mouth told him she was teasing and trying to hide a smile.

Suddenly he felt a little less hollow.

"That's providing all the babies cooperate." Again, he hesitated, but her reaction had seemed to lower the wall she'd erected between them by a few inches. "How did you take hearing the news you were having the triplets?"

"About as well as you did."

"It was that obvious, huh?"

"Oh, yeah." Her gaze met his then lowered again to her belly. "It's a lot to deal with at once. Overwhelming. But exciting."

"And scary."

"And scary," she echoed.

And she would have to face every overwhelming, exciting, scary step all on her own.

On her own except for her grandma and all their friends, as she had been sure to tell him when she had said she didn't need him along for the ride. That was okay with him. He hadn't signed on for a ride like this one. He only wanted her to agree to take help from him, and then he'd be out of here, his obligation fulfilled and Cowboy Creek in his rearview mirror.

His hand slipped again. No scratch this time, but it was a close call. He wiped his palm on his jeans. "I need to get out. To the truck. For another screwdriver. The tools they give you with an assembly kit don't always do the best job."

"All right." One hand on her back, she made her way to the doorway ahead of him. "I think I'm going to go and put my feet up for just a minute."

He watched as she moved down the hallway, her pace so slow and steady no one could have noticed anything awkward or ungainly about her progress. Probably no one would even realize she was pregnant and carrying three babies.

He knew. And that hand at the small of her back bothered him more than he could say.

He went down the stairs to the first floor at about Shay's speed, his thoughts still upstairs with her. She was independent, not a bad trait to have and one he hoped she passed along to the kids. But as for that danged stubbornness—

He hadn't yet made it to the front door when she called his name, her voice shrill.

Frowning, he about-faced and went up the stairs again at a run. The hallway was empty. He didn't know where she had gone. As he passed the babies' bedroom, she called him again.

Third door on the left, into a smaller bedroom. She sat on the edge of the bed with her arm cradling her belly. After one look, he went down on his knee beside her and took her free hand. It was shaking. Or maybe that was his. "What's wrong?"

"I don't know," she said, her voice still high. "I'm having pains."

"Hey, hey, calm down," he said soothingly, he hoped. "It's not too soon for the babies to come, is it?"

"No. We were hoping they would hold out a bit longer, but my doctors told me I could go into labor at any time. It's just..." She swallowed hard. "I'm scheduled to deliver in Santa Fe."

"And maybe you still will. Everything will be all right." How would he know? But when she nodded, seeming calmer, he was glad he had given her the reassurance. "Why don't you call your doctor and let him know what's going on."

She nodded. "My cell phone. It's in my bag. I think I left it on the couch when we came in."

"I remember. Be right back." He strode along the hall and took the stairs three at a time. He'd told her to calm down, but who was there to say that to him? As he grabbed the bag, he stole the time to take one steadying breath before going back up the stairs. It wouldn't help Shay if he fell all to pieces.

She must have had the doctor on speed dial, because in seconds she was talking to someone on the other end of the line, explaining about the pains. Even as she described them, another one seemed to hit her. She gasped but kept her attention on the conversation. He paced the room, wondering how he would handle it if she had the babies right now.

A few moments later, midsentence, she grabbed at her stomach and slammed the phone on the bed.

He took the cell from her and spoke into it. "My name's Tyler. I'm…here visiting with Shay. What should we do?"

A reassuringly steady voice said, "This is Dr. Grayden. Have Shay lie down with her feet up. We're sending an ambulance to her address. It's already on the way."

"Are the *babies* on the way?"

"I won't know that until I see Shay."

He must have mumbled something, because the doctor said kindly, "Don't worry, young man. Once the ambulance arrives, she'll be in good hands with the EMTs and then with the staff at the hospital. Until that time, you're to tell her she's in equally good hands. Yours. Keep her calm and relaxed and remind her to practice her deep breathing. Understood?"

"Understood."

"Good. I'll be waiting when you arrive."

He disconnected the call. Shay stared at him, wide-eyed. He took her hand. "It's okay," he said firmly. "They've got an ambulance on the way. You're supposed to lie down and practice breathing."

Nodding, she lay back against the bed. He lifted her feet so she could stretch out comfortably.

"Want a blanket?"

"No, I'm fine. But I'm supposed to be having the babies in Santa Fe," she said again. "That's where the specialist is. That's where they have the high-risk NICU."

High risk? No wonder she was in such a panic. He took another deep breath. "Dr. Grayden says you'll be in good hands at the hospital here." He didn't tell her what the doc had said about *his* capabilities in the meantime. With luck, the man was right about that, too.

"I know," she agreed, "but this isn't what we expected to happen. One of the babies is turned. I can't deliver. I'm supposed to have a C-section."

"And you will," he said as soothingly as he could. "They can deliver the babies here in Cowboy Creek, can't they?"

She shrugged. "The specialist said they have a special care unit at our hospital. And a nurse on staff trained to handle multiple births."

"Then the hospital's on alert and ready, right? And remember, you told me the doctor said anything can happen as far as the timing. Maybe the babies are just tired of waiting and eager to get here."

She gave a half laugh that made his heart flip. "Not as eager as I am."

"Well, then, that's what we'll keep thinking." He squeezed her hand slightly.

As another pain hit, she moaned and gripped his fingers.

Chapter Nine

Chasing an ambulance to Cowboy Creek General Hospital was another ride Tyler hadn't signed on for. Driving white-knuckled and leaning over the steering wheel hadn't helped to make the trip any shorter.

The ambulance had seemed to take forever to arrive at the house. In reality, the clock on Shay's cell phone when he dropped it into her bag showed only eleven minutes had passed since she'd called her doctor. One of the benefits of living in a small town.

One of the drawbacks was now staring him in the face, her expression stern and forbidding above her nurse's uniform. She was half his size and judging by her gray curls probably three times his age, and still she held the power to stop him in his tracks. "I'm sorry, but as I've told you twice already, no one but the designated support person is allowed beyond this point."

"But I followed Shay here in the ambulance," he protested.

"I'm sorry."

"I have her bag." He held it up as if it were a talisman that would magically grant him entrance through the doors just yards away.

"I'll see the family is notified when they get here."

"When will that be?" His voice had risen a few notches in frustration. The nurse frowned at him. He glared back. He wanted to throttle the woman. He wanted to push past her and go down the hallway and through the automatic doors into the bowels of the hospital, to wherever he would find Shay.

In the minutes they had waited for the ambulance to arrive at the house, then for the medical techs to transfer her onto a stretcher and downstairs and into the emergency vehicle, she'd had a few more pains or contractions or whatever they might have been. The anguish on her face just before they'd closed the ambulance doors had torn at his heart.

That was the last he'd seen of her, and now this dragon of a hospital employee was keeping him from seeing Shay again, turning down his requests to talk to her doctor, refusing to let him know her status.

But these are my kids *she's having*, he wanted to snap at her.

The knowledge finally hit, a solid blow that almost sent him staggering.

Yes, Shay was bringing these lives into the world. But no matter what she said, they were his as much as hers. Not just his responsibility. His *family*.

The nurse took him by the arm, urging him away from the admittance desk. His heart lightened at the knowledge she was finally going to take pity on him. Instead, she led him aside and nearly backed him up against a wall, most likely, he belatedly realized, to get him as far away as possible from the curious stares of everyone else in the room.

"You're not listed on our paperwork as the father of

record or even a close family member." She gave him a small, malicious smile. "Therefore, I'm not allowed to divulge any further information to you."

Of course not. Why should she be allowed to do that when she wouldn't do anything else?

Then the implications of what she had said sank in. She wasn't allowed to divulge any further information to him. He wasn't listed in Shay's records. Did that mean she had named someone *else* as the father?

The dragon turned and walked away.

He glanced around him. Everyone in the place sat staring at him as if *he* were the dragon. One with six heads.

Suddenly he felt grateful for the wall behind his back. He sagged against it and ran his hand over his face. The evil nurse might have control at the moment, but somehow he needed to get information from her. Acting like a real jackass wasn't going to get him anywhere. Desperately, he searched for a single sane thought to hold on to—and couldn't find one. Every thought he had was jumbled, erratic and fleeting.

He'd never planned to become a daddy. Never wanted to be a daddy. And yet, here he was, in a panic because that's exactly what was going to happen, and that dragon nurse was telling him *he had no rights to his own children.*

Now she stood with her back to him calmly flipping through a few charts on the desk in front of her. He was tempted to vault over the front counter and tear across the space behind her and through the double doors.

That idea was put to rest when the automatic doors from the street swished open and Grandma Mo entered the emergency room with Jed Garland at her side.

TYLER HAD LOST track of time.

He and Jed had taken seats while Mo stopped at the counter, evidently to provide the staff with all kinds of information he wouldn't have known. He leaned forward, face tilted down, elbows on his knees, in an attempt both to avoid the continuing stares of those around him and to get his head together again.

Eventually, Mo returned to lead them both down the hall to a family waiting room. Lightly padded plastic chairs made a corral around a low table holding some magazines and a few books.

He tried to get comfortable in this awkward situation. Jed knew the truth. But did Mo know who had fathered her granddaughter's babies?

He told them what had happened back at the house, describing Shay's pains, the phone call, the arrival of the ambulance.

The nurse, whose name turned out to be Annabel, entered the room with a tray of paper cups filled with water. "Cafeteria's closed for the night, but I thought y'all might like something to drink."

Sitting had put him at about eye level with her. He couldn't avoid meeting her gaze. As she handed him a cup, she gave him the same small smile she'd given him earlier, which he now could see didn't have a trace of malice in it. Instead, it was a sympathetic smile. She wasn't a dragon nurse after all.

Panic could make a man think crazy things.

"Sorry about before," he muttered, taking the cup.

She patted his shoulder. "Most men aren't at their best when they show up here with a woman in labor."

Yeah, but how many of those men were daddies with three babies arriving at once? And could the fact he would soon face just that event excuse some of his behavior?

As for the staring faces in the waiting room, he didn't know whether it helped or hurt that, very likely, those were all folks who knew Shay—and Mo and Jed. Just as likely, they were all thrilled to finally have a look at a potential candidate for the father of Shay's babies.

Jed and Mo sat watching him. Grandma Mo hadn't said a word about his panic. More importantly, she hadn't reacted to Annabel's reassurances, which answered his question about whether or not she knew the truth about him. Either she'd known all along, or the surprisingly kindly nurse had clued Mo in when they were filling out hospital forms together.

As Annabel left them, he took a gulp of water, then looked at Mo.

Green eyes almost the shade of Shay's stared back at him.

"You know?" he asked.

She nodded.

"Shay told you?"

She shook her head. "No, it was more a case of putting two and two together."

"Or two and three, as it's turned out."

She gave a soft laugh. "That it has. Never did I think I'd be having my great-grandchildren by the handful. I'm happy for it. But I'll be happier once I know they're all here and healthy."

"That makes a few of us." He hesitated, then admitted, "I kind of went off the deep end when the nurse wouldn't let me know what was going on with Shay."

Jed settled back in his chair and stretched his legs out in front of him. "I was in that position when my

Mary and I had our first boy. Sometimes, with all the hustle and bustle and everybody knowing their jobs and doing them, it feels like the daddy's the last to learn the details."

"My husband felt the same when I delivered Shay's father," Mo said. "It's no shame that you felt a bit frustrated, Tyler, when Annabel wouldn't answer your questions. If it's any consolation, she said you were almost persuasive enough to make her bend the rules."

"Obnoxious enough, she means."

"Well," Mo said, her eyes twinkling, "that *may* have been one of the words she used."

He sent her a rueful grin.

The doors to the waiting room opened again. A silver-haired man wearing a white coat and a wide smile came directly to Mo.

"Everything's fine," he said promptly, to Tyler's immediate relief. That feeling disappeared just as quickly when the man, his expression now solemn, took a seat beside Mo and rested his hand on her shoulder. "We're not going to be able to transfer Shay and the babies up to Santa Fe as planned."

"But you're prepared for the births here, Jim?" she asked. Tension ratcheted up the accent he'd noticed in her voice.

"You already know we are, Mo. Now, don't worry about that."

"What about her pain?" Tyler demanded.

The doctor glanced at him, then back to Mo again. She nodded as if confirming she wanted the information, too.

"We don't have a definitive answer for that yet," the doctor told him. He returned his attention to Mo. "All four of them are being monitored closely while we run some tests. The babies' lung development has already been checked, and everything is just as it should be. The tests will tell us if there's anything more. From everything we've seen so far, in my and my colleague's opinions, the babies are getting restless."

He smiled, and Tyler liked the man for trying to ease Mo's worry.

"When we have any news," he continued, "you'll be the first to know. Once the testing is done, you may be allowed in to see her. You alone, but it may be a while."

She nodded. "I'll be right here."

"Good." The doctor nodded to Tyler and Jed, then left.

"Well, son," Jed said, "looks like it might be time for us to go home."

Stalling, Tyler pretended to take a drink from his already empty cup.

Shay wouldn't acknowledge his rights. The nurse wasn't allowed to accept his word. The doctor addressed all his comments to Shay's grandma. And it looked like Jed wanted him to walk away.

That left Mo, who sat quietly watching him.

"I'll stay for a bit," he told Jed. "You've got a way to get back to the ranch?"

"Got my truck. Don't worry about that."

The echo of the doctor's words to Mo made Tyler think again of Shay. And her pain. And their conversation at the Big Dipper when he found he was going to become the father of three.

It's not up to you who I tell and who I don't.

He winced, sure he knew how she would feel about him discussing her with her grandma. But there was nothing he could do about that now. And it was the least of his worries.

Mo sat with her head tilted, studying him thoughtfully. He'd bet her next words wouldn't make him feel any better.

"Since we can't tell how long I'll be sitting here," she started, "and as Dr. Grayden said I'm to be the only one allowed in to see Shay…"

The only one Shay wanted to see.

The cup he held seemed to vibrate in his hand. Slowly, he curled his fingers around it, crumpling it in his fist. He tossed it into a trash basket near the end of the couch.

Mo continued gently, "In view of the circumstances, Tyler, I think it might be best for you to go with Jed. I'll be in touch when I know something."

Jed clapped him on the shoulder as if to second her request.

Looked like no one thought he had the right to be here.

Chapter Ten

"Your babies are beautiful."

At Layne's enthusiastic assessment, Shay couldn't hold back a grin. In the two days since she had given birth, she hadn't been able to stop smiling. Other than informing her the babies had a case of jaundice, Dr. Grayden had pronounced them perfect.

Even the exhaustion from two days and nights of sleep broken by multiple feedings couldn't dim her happiness. Her babies were safe and sound, healthy, and finally *here*.

She looked at the small cribs lined up against one wall of the hospital's neonatal care room. "Thanks. I think they're beautiful, too, but it's good to hear it confirmed by an expert mommy."

Layne laughed. "I'm no expert. And according to Mo, you're doing fine yourself."

"So are the babies. We should be able to move into a room together soon. Right now they're here under a special light to help with their jaundice. Dr. Grayden says they may need to stay an extra day in the hospital because of that, but their color is improving. And they all have great appetites."

"I thought they looked bigger already," Layne teased. She had seen the triplets for the first time the day before.

"They *are* bigger. Timothy met the minimum birth weight to go home. Jamie was just under the wire, but he's above it now, too. And Bree has only a few ounces to go before she catches up with her big brothers. I'm having to supplement with bottle feedings. It wasn't my first choice, but…"

"Nothing wrong with that. You wouldn't have enough milk to nurse three babies," Layne said matter-of-factly.

"That's true. They do seem to eat a lot. And when they're not eating, they pretty much spend their time sleeping."

"Be grateful for that," Layne advised. "In just a few days, you'll be wishing for more nap times."

"For them or for me?"

"Both."

They laughed.

"I know Mo's been here," Layne said. "Sugar and Beth told me they stopped in, too."

"I'm glad to have the company." Dr. Grayden and the staff were all business when it came to watching over her babies, and she couldn't have asked for better care even from the neonatal unit in Santa Fe. There, visitors might not yet have been allowed, but in a small-town hospital like Cowboy Creek's, the rules were more flexible.

"Has anyone from the ranch been to see you?" Layne asked.

"Yes, Jed and Paz were here yesterday after you left, and Tina and Jane were in this morning." Layne continued to look at her expectantly. Shay frowned. "I know what you're thinking, and the answer's no."

Layne gave a small gasp of surprise. "But now Tyler knows he's the daddy. He didn't even make an attempt to get here?"

"Not as far as I know. Witnessing my panic at the house the other day must have given him a big dose of reality. And watching me being taken away in the ambulance probably made him think about the craziness of life with three babies. No wonder he hasn't come to the hospital." She shrugged. "That's fine with me. I don't want to see him. And the babies are too little even to notice who visits them."

But were they? In just these two days, all three of her babies had bonded with her. They appeared comfortable when Grandma and Paz and Jed held them. They seemed quick to respond to anyone who came into their very small world. But of course, they couldn't miss someone they'd never known.

Layne said nothing.

"I know what you're thinking again, but he doesn't have any right to be here. He doesn't plan to be…anything to my babies." She looked away from Layne and focused on the cribs. "Grandma and Jed are stopping by this afternoon. They'll be here soon. Please promise me you won't bring up Tyler's name in front of them."

"Tyler who?" Layne asked airily.

Shay laughed, but somehow, she didn't trust that tone.

No matter what excuses she had just made, she had been surprised that Tyler hadn't shown up at some point during visiting hours. He had been with her when she'd gone into labor. He had held her hand and tried to calm her while they waited for the EMTs. Even in the hustle of her transfer to the ambulance, she recalled him in the background, lending her silent support. She had thought for sure he would want to see their babies.

But that was just wishful thinking. She needed to stop those crazy thoughts. As she had told Layne, he didn't intend to have anything to do with the triplets.

She felt the same about him. And to her relief, it looked like he had walked out of her life again for good.

IN THE HOSPITAL parking lot, Jed held the door of his truck open until Mo settled herself inside. Then he went around to the driver's door and climbed in to sit beside her. Even if he hadn't volunteered to pick her up from her house and take her home again, he'd have come to see Shay and her little ones, just like he had with Tina when his first great-grandson had been born in this very hospital, too. For him, new life was a sight that never got old.

"Your girl seemed more restless this afternoon than she did yesterday," he said. "What did you think?"

"I agree. She'll be wanting to get those babies home."

"And something else?"

Mo tilted her head, considering. "I've not quite figured her out yet, Jed. She hasn't said a word to me about Tyler. Has she mentioned him to you?"

"Nope. Nor to Paz. More than likely she doesn't want to make a fuss. She doesn't ask about Cole or Pete or Mitch, except in general. If she singled Tyler out, how would she explain her interest in him, since she doesn't know *we* know why she's interested?"

Mo frowned. "It's a good thing I know how your mind works after all these years, Jed Garland, or I'd never have understood a word you just said."

He laughed. "You know darned well your mind's

working just the same as mine. Now…once Shay gets home with those babies, we need to make sure she and Tyler have plenty of time alone with them."

"I don't see how that can happen. Our schedule's already full with women who have volunteered to come in to help."

"Schedules often change, Mo."

She smiled. "That's true enough, isn't it. And until then? I haven't a clue in my head as to what to do next."

"That's just it."

"What is?"

"We don't do anything next. We let nature take its course." He gestured toward the hospital. "Shay's been in here for a couple of days now, and I've got everybody at the Hitching Post staying quiet about how she's doing. I figure the less we say to Tyler, the easier it'll be to flush him out."

"Meaning…?"

"Meaning he can't show his hand by asking too much about Shay, either. But I don't think he'll be able to hold out much longer. Eventually, he's going to talk to me outright about her."

"And what are you going to tell him?"

Grinning, he started the pickup. "Haven't got a clue in my head."

Tyler parked his truck in the hospital lot between two cars only half its size. He hadn't wanted to come. Shay wouldn't want to see him. She wouldn't even admit to anyone he had fathered her babies. And still, here he was.

He had lasted three days. Three long days of hearing the Garlands talk about Shay and the kids without revealing much of anything new. Three frustrating days of learning next to nothing after Paz and Jed's visits to the hospital. Three anxious days without knowing how Shay was doing, other than Jed's uncharacteristically brief reports of "fine."

"Fine" didn't tell him anything.

The rest of the Garlands had to know he was the babies' dad, but it was as if they were deliberately shutting him out. He couldn't ask questions, couldn't show too much interest. Not after he'd made a point of telling Jed he had no plans of marrying Shay.

But what if they all were trying to hide something from him? Maybe that ride in the ambulance hadn't been good for her or the babies. Maybe something he'd said or done had upset her enough to make her go into labor early.

He needed to satisfy himself she really was okay, to obliterate the memory of his last sight of her—of her agonized face as the medics loaded her into the ambulance. Somehow, the fact he had witnessed her panic in that ambulance made him feel responsible for it. The fact he couldn't do anything for her had left him feeling helpless.

She'd had plenty of visitors since she had been checked into the hospital. The Garlands had said that much, and they'd mentioned that the staff was taking excellent care of her. She and the babies were in good hands. Still, he needed to see that for himself. Just once.

Inside the hospital, he made his way to the reception desk.

"Shay O'Neill," he said.

From memory, the teenage volunteer recited the room number and gave him directions for finding it.

He considered himself lucky Shay hadn't left his name and description at the front desk along with a caution to the staff to keep him from visiting her.

After he'd pushed the call button for the elevator, he stared down at his hands. They were trembling. Worse, maybe, they were empty.

On the other side of the lobby he spotted the sign for the hospitality shop. Flowers, candy, stuffed animals and balloons filled the shelves inside. He could take his pick.

A stuffed tiger and a lion, both sporting blue bows, seemed to call to him to take them from the shelf. He also chose a plush gray elephant wearing a big pink-and-white-striped neck ruffle. At the last moment, he grabbed a large ceramic mug with a couple of balloons tied to the handle and "Mom" stenciled in both pink and blue multiple times around the outside.

"This looks just right for the new mother of a few kids, doesn't it," he said to the clerk at the register.

"Shay will love it."

Stunned, he stared at her. Maybe his description *had* been circulated throughout the hospital. After all, the day Shay had been brought here, no one had wanted him hanging around. Not Annabel. Not Mo or Jed. And especially not Shay.

Then he realized…small town, small hospital, three babies. It couldn't have been a stretch for the clerk to figure out his reference to a mother with multiple kids.

He left the shop with his arms full, refusing to admit even to himself that he needed all this as an excuse for his visit.

When he reached the room, he felt immensely thankful to have something to hold on to. He spotted Shay first, sitting in a padded chair with wooden arms and legs. Her wheat-blond hair was ruffled, as if she'd rested her head against the chair for a nap. He wanted to reach out and smooth the strands into place. Instead, he clutched his peace offerings.

She seemed sleepy, her attention unfocused—until she registered him standing in the doorway. She said nothing, which made him doubly glad to have something to do with his unsteady hands.

She glanced past him to the doorway, maybe hoping someone would come along to kick him out. Then she stared across the room, as if searching for an answer from the babies. Finally, she looked back at him.

"Hey," he said, raising his purchases slightly. "I'm in charge of the new-baby welcome wagon." Stupidest remark he'd ever made. And yet his heart lightened when her lips curled slightly in a reluctant one-sided smile. "How are you doing?"

"Okay."

That didn't tell him much more than "fine."

"Are you sleeping all right?"

"Sleep? What's that?"

At least she still had a sense of humor. "Eating okay?"

She nodded. "I have to, since I'm feeding three."

"So." He cleared his throat. "Mind if I come in?"

"You already have."

It wasn't the warmest reply he might have gotten, but it would have to do. A look around him proved, sure enough, he had edged a step into the room. He couldn't back out now.

"Thought you might like this." He gestured with the mug and crossed the space between them to set it on the small table beside her. The balloons scuttled sideways above them like clouds in a driving wind.

"Thanks."

Smiling, he shrugged and held up the animals. "Didn't want anybody feeling left out."

She nodded, her eyes suddenly glistening.

Just as suddenly, he couldn't think of another thing to say.

Over against one wall, three cribs stood in a row.

"Want to take a peek?" she asked.

His throat tightened, and now he couldn't have spoken even if he'd come up with something else to discuss. Jed and Paz had said the babies were in a special room of their own. He hadn't thought about seeing them here. He didn't intend to walk over to them. But when a new mom sat looking at you the way Shay looked at him, you really didn't have a choice.

He clutched the stuffed animals, took a deep breath and nodded. As he took his first steps across the room, his legs threatened to give way. He attempted to tread lightly, not wanting the sound of his boots clomping on the tile floor to startle the occupants of the cribs.

He needn't have worried. They all looked sound asleep.

His throat tightened another notch. The babies were tinier than he'd expected and wrapped in blankets, blue for the boys and a pink one for the girl. He had heard Paz tell Tina and Jane their names and the order of their births. The same as the order of their cribs, with each name posted on a plastic card at the headboard.

Timothy. Jamie. Bree.

Gripping the stuffed animals, he looked down at the babies again.

Jamie and Bree lay curled up, completely covered and apparently comfortable in their blankets. Big brother Timothy had worked one hand free. On the edge of the blanket he had rested his fist, no bigger than a walnut and just about as wrinkled.

The sight of that fist, of the babies themselves, suddenly made it hard for him to catch his breath.

"They…uh…they've had jaundice," Shay said softly.

He hadn't heard her come up beside him. "They're—" His voice cracked. He tried again. "They're okay, though? They'll get over that?"

She nodded. "They're better now."

"When do you get to take them home?"

"Dr. Grayden says if all goes well with their check-ups tomorrow morning, he'll release them then."

"That's good."

"Yes." She paused. "I appreciate all you did…the other day."

He nodded.

They stood beside each other, staring down at the cribs.

Finally, she sighed. "Well…thank you for the gifts," she said stiffly. Formally. In a tone meant to tell him his visit had ended.

He gestured with the toys in his arms. "What should I do with these? Put them in the cribs?"

She shook her head. "No, I don't think the nurses would go for that." A moment later, she said, "Maybe you should leave them at the Hitching Post. I can pick them up from there."

After you've gone.

That's what she meant. This time, both her tone and her expression got her message across. "You don't want me here, do you?"

She didn't answer. Her silence bothered him. He hadn't intended to stay once he'd seen her. He had only wanted to satisfy himself she was all right. He had done that now, hadn't he? And yet he didn't move. This stand-off reminded him of the day he had first come to the hospital.

"When they brought you in, I followed you," he blurted. "Followed the ambulance, I mean. They wouldn't let me ride with you. Downstairs, they wouldn't tell me what was going on. Not a word about how you were doing. Nothing about the babies' conditions. They shut me out, as if I had no rights at all."

For a moment, her expression froze. Her eyes seem to dull. She took a deep breath and sighed again. "I don't understand," she said finally, pacing her words. "You've already told me you don't want to be a father. You don't want a family. So why would it matter to you? Why do you even care about rights?"

Chapter Eleven

Tyler must not have realized how upset he had sounded. For a long moment Shay teetered on the brink of believing he cared about her and the babies more than he wanted her to know. After all, there he stood holding an armful of gifts for the triplets. Then she weighed her belief against what he had said that night at the Big Dipper.

Evidently her reminder about his not wanting kids or a family had hit home. Now, he said nothing. Her slim hope he had changed his mind disappeared as rapidly as the light left his eyes.

"You've got a point," he said.

"I thought so."

"But that doesn't do away with my obligations."

From the hallway, the rattle of a hospital cart on the tile flooring alerted her that Patsy, the day nurse, was on her way into the room. "You should go," she said quickly. "Morning visiting hours will be ending soon."

"I didn't hear an announcement."

"They don't broadcast that over the speakers in this wing. It's intensive care. But visits here are limited."

Patsy entered the room, pushing the cart ahead of her. "Lunchtime," she announced. "Ah, I see we have someone new to help today. Won't that be nice?"

Shay forced a smile. "He's just leaving."

From pure contrariness, she was sure, Tyler smiled at the nurse. Or maybe he had the reaction so practiced, he never had to think about it twice. The grandmotherly nurse responded to his playboy smile the way *she* had done at first sight, too—like a teenager in danger of breaking out in giggles at the attention of a cute boy.

"No, I'm not leaving yet." He set the animals on the edge of her bed. "Happy to lend a hand. What can I do? Clear off the table for Mom's lunch tray?"

And yes, Patsy giggled. "It's not Mom who's eating now, it's the babies."

The look of alarm on Tyler's face almost made up for his insistence on sticking around. Almost. He had been right a few minutes ago—she didn't want him here.

For their maternity patients, the hospital allowed a spouse more visiting time. If she had listed him as the father on her admittance forms, he could have been with her and the babies most of the day. As she had a private room, he could have stayed overnight. Her heart hurt at the loss of too many could-haves.

"Since I don't see any other visitors," Patsy went on, "I'm sure Mom will appreciate your help. So will I. Three babies are too much for one person to handle alone, and I've got to go check on a new patient we've just admitted. So let's get this assembly line going. Shall we start with Timothy, Shay, since he's always the one most interested in his bottle?"

"Yes," she said, trying to sound cheerful. Trying for the babies' sakes not to get upset.

As much as she longed to toss Tyler out of her room, she didn't dare. He had agreed with her point about his not caring about her babies. But he had pushed the issue about his obligations. If she spoke up, she wouldn't put it past him to claim his parental rights here and now.

Patsy wheeled the cart close to the bedside table and transferred the babies' bottles. Then she turned her attention back to him. "Your name is…"

"Tyler."

"All right, then, Tyler. Follow my lead. All you'll be required to do is carry the babies back and forth from their beds. Mom does all the rest."

She went to Timothy's crib. "Now, just in case you've never been told, what's most important with the little ones, infants especially, is that you support their heads. Both with lifting and while holding the babies. Like this." After her demonstration, she reached up to hand the baby to Tyler.

He took the infant hesitantly, then seemed at a loss.

Patsy laughed. "It's all right. Most people are a bit nervous the first few times they handle a newborn."

With her assistance, he held the baby in one arm. Tyler's height and the breadth of his shoulders made the blue-wrapped bundle appear even tinier against the black T-shirt snugly fitting his chest. The look of concentration on his face, his slight frown as he adjusted his hold, the careful way he crossed the room as if afraid he might drop her son, all made Shay's vision blur.

Blinking her eyes rapidly, she kept her head down and her gaze focused on Timothy as Tyler transferred him to her arms. Tyler's hands looked so big and sturdy as they cradled the baby, felt so warm as they brushed hers. He seemed so in control.

She couldn't believe that, though, considering he'd

held her son for less than a minute. Just as she couldn't believe in him. This was all a playboy pose for the nurse's benefit.

"HAVE YOU HAD a good day, lass?" Grandma asked when she arrived for the afternoon visiting hour.

"A *very* good day," Shay said. "Dr. Grayden stopped in to see the babies. He said chances are still good we'll go home after the checkups tomorrow."

"Good. The house is quiet without you."

She laughed. "Enjoy it while you can, Grandma. I don't think it will ever be quiet again."

"And that's not such a bad thing, is it?"

"Not at all."

"You've had other visitors?"

Automatically, Shay's gaze went to the Mom mug with its colorful balloons and, beside it, the three stuffed animals. The toys sat in a row on the windowsill, a reminder of her babies lined up in their cribs. She had spent too much time this afternoon staring at those gifts. Resolutely, she looked away.

"Layne stopped in on her way to work, at the beginning of this afternoon's visiting hours." Feeling guilty, she slid past a mention of the visitor who'd arrived after Grandma had left this morning. But the fewer people who knew about him, the better.

Tyler had stayed longer than she had expected, long enough for her to feed all three babies and for him to tuck them back into their cribs. She had planned to tell him she could handle Bree, who would be the last to eat, so that he could be on his way. But at that point, Patsy had bustled back into the room to check on her tiny patients.

He had made a big show of his expertise in carrying Jamie back to his crib and resettling him, then bringing Bree to Shay, all under Patsy's smiling approval.

She held back a sigh. The day he had insisted on helping to set up the babies' room, he had claimed that, after he left Cowboy Creek again, he would send her money for the babies. Seeing him here this morning had only made her wish he wanted to do much more. Yet, she knew better than to expect anything from him.

She looked up to see Grandma watching her and realized her thoughts had distracted her for too long. "You just missed Layne by a few minutes," she said quickly.

"I'll see her at SugarPie's later. Now, I hope you won't be too upset, but I've made arrangements to meet a few of the girls for supper. I may not make it back in time to visit with you tonight."

"That's fine. I'm going to try to nap as much as I can between feedings today. It won't be as easy for me to sleep once I'm home again."

"I'll be there to help, of course."

"Oh, I know you will. But I can't take up all your time. You've got so much going on."

"And what could be more important than taking care of my own great-grandbabies?"

"What about the knitting circle, and the bridge club, and everything else?"

"They rank far down the list after babies one, two and three." Mo smiled. "Don't worry, lass, we'll work things out. And we've got all the ladies coming in to help us."

For the first few weeks, they would have daily hands-on assistance and the delivery of home-cooked meals from friends. After that, they had made plans to alternate their time with the babies so Shay could get back to work. Despite Grandma's telling her not to worry… she worried. Not that Grandma couldn't handle a baby on her own. But they were talking *three* babies.

Even as their mom, she wasn't sure how she would manage, but saying so might add to Grandma's unspoken concerns.

Luckily, she had other outlets for sharing her worries. Between Layne and Tina and Tina's cousin Andi, she would have plenty of people to go to when she needed to ask advice…at least, when it came to babies.

ONE OF SHAY'S biggest worries showed up again for the evening visiting hours. When she heard a familiar tread in the hallway approaching her room, she closed her eyes in dismay, somehow hoping that not being able to see Tyler would mean he had disappeared.

When she opened her eyes again, he stood in the doorway, nearly filling it. Instantly, she thought of the first moment she had seen him, the day of Tina and Cole's wedding, dressed in a tux with a deep blue tie and cummerbund that made his eyes even bluer. He had walked through the doorway into the Hitching Post's small chapel looking so tall, so dark-haired and handsome. So *hot*. Now, she felt that same larger-than-life sensation and a powerful fluttering in her stomach.

"Did I wake you?" he asked.

She blinked, trying to chase the images and feelings away. "No. I was just…resting my eyes."

"Babies awake?"

"They have been, off and on."

He hung his Stetson on the corner of the extra visitor's chair. Then he took the other, quietly pulling it too close to her bed for comfort. So close she could see things she didn't want to see. This late in the day, his jaw sported a five-o'clock shadow, a dark growth she knew would feel prickly-soft against her fingertips.

He had changed into a long-sleeved white Western shirt that made his eyes look as blue as sapphires. The shirt brought back more memories she didn't want. She had once opened a shirt just like that one, snap by snap, planning to take it off him. But he'd turned the tables, reaching for the buttons on her blouse.

"You sure you're not sleeping?"

Starting, she blinked hard, then cleared her throat. "I'm awake. Wh-what are you doing here?"

"Jed was missing from the table at the Hitching Post tonight. Tina said he'd made plans with Mo for supper at SugarPie's."

She frowned. "Grandma's supposed to be meeting some of her friends. Female friends."

He shrugged. "Well, I guess Jed got himself invited along."

"That wouldn't take much," she agreed.

"Since they're tied up, I thought you might need an extra pair of hands. Have I missed the rounds tonight?"

"No. I expect at least one of the babies to wake up and be ready to eat soon."

"Good. Having three kids to practice with has made me feel like I've passed a crash course. In fact, I think I'm due for some kind of merit badge."

She lost the fight not to smile. "I have to admit, I think I need one, too. *And* a medal for stamina. Between feeding and diapering, I've been putting one baby down only to pick up the next one."

"Like a merry-go-round that doesn't stop."

"Just like that," she said, surprised at how accurately he'd described what she had been feeling.

She should tell him to go. Patsy would soon be here with the bottles for the evening feeding, and the babies would awaken, and again she would have to see Tyler hold them close and carry them to her. Watching him this morning had been heart wrenching. She didn't want to have to face that again. She didn't want her babies to get used to having him around.

"Time for a bed check?" He tilted his head toward the cribs.

She hesitated, then gave in, only because she would never turn down a chance to look at her babies. "Let's go and see." Dr. Grayden had given his okay for her to get up and moving. In fact, her good progress was a deciding factor for her upcoming release from the hospital. She pushed aside the sheet covering her and stood.

Her eagerness had nothing to do with walking beside Tyler, with standing beside him in front of the cribs and looking down at the babies they had brought into the world. It had nothing to do with wanting to lean into his warmth and let him wrap his arms around her. Nothing to do with wishing, just for a few minutes, that being with their babies would somehow instantly make them a family.

After a moment, he reached down to touch Timothy's hand. "There's that fist again. Looks like this one's going to be a fighter."

"He'll need to be when he has to stick up for his little brother and sister."

"They ought to learn to do that for themselves."

"Well, yes. But it will be good for Jamie and Bree to have a protector if the schoolyard bullies start pushing them around. I didn't have any brothers or sisters to do that for me."

"Me, either. I didn't have anybody sticking up for me when I was a kid."

"Except your parents, you mean. The way Grandma did for me."

He laughed shortly. "My parents were the last ones to have my back. My father would tell me to fight my own battles, then push me outside again to 'face down my fears.' And my mom went right along with that."

"When you were still in school?"

"Yeah. High school. Grade school. Kindergarten."

"That's awful."

"That's my old man for you."

No wonder Tyler had talked about children becoming independent the minute they became adults. He had never known what it was like to receive a parent's un-conditional love, the way she did from Grandma. Then again, he might be viewing his father from the perspec-tive of a grade schooler or kindergartner.

"Maybe," she said, "in his eyes, he was helping you. Maybe trying to—"

"Trying to make a man out of me? Yeah, so he said. I hope that's not the way you plan to go about it with the kids." As if he felt uncomfortable, he looked back at the babies. "Anyway, these three were only born a few minutes apart from each other. Who's to say Bree won't be the leader of the pack? Equal rights from nurs-ery school on."

She laughed. "I like that idea."

A smile played on his lips, softening the hard lines of his shadowed jaw. She liked that, too.

Sobering, she looked down at the babies again. She

didn't want to like anything about Tyler. She didn't want to see anything else that would bring back memories they had shared. But that was an impossible wish.

With a sigh, she stroked the small patch of hair atop Bree's head. The color wasn't as dark as Tyler's. But like her brothers', Bree's brown fluff was already much darker than Shay's blond hair. Chances were, all the babies would eventually have a shade much closer to Tyler's rich, dark brown.

She would always have visual reminders of him, whether or not she wanted them—and she didn't. A few minutes of feeling closer to him couldn't make up for the fact he chose not to stay.

Chapter Twelve

After an early breakfast at the Hitching Post, Tyler left the hotel. The sun was already bright, promising a warm day. Long, empty hours stretched ahead of him, and he planned a ride to fill up some of that time. He couldn't have described his surroundings, could never have found his way back to the hotel later on, if not for Freedom. He trusted the stallion to be his eyes and ears.

More than once, he had acknowledged he'd long passed the point he should have headed back to Texas. That wasn't going to happen while he had unfinished business here.

He returned from his ride midmorning, and had just settled Freedom in his stall again when Cole came into the barn.

"Tyler, we meet at last. You're making a real habit of disappearing. I went to the dining room for break-fast, and Jed said you had eaten already. And when I finished reading Robbie a story after supper last night, I couldn't find you anywhere."

"Keeping tabs on me?"

"No. But it looks like I might have to start, just to make sure you stay out of trouble. Where'd you run off to last night?"

"The hospital." During the evening visiting hours, his conversation with Shay about the babies had given him the feeling he had made a degree of progress at winning her over, that he had taken one step down the road to making her understand he was serious about helping her...financially.

"How are Shay and the kids? Tina went into town to see them the other day and said those babies are really something. Then again, she says that about every kid."

"They *are* something, all three of them. Cutest babies I've ever seen." Not that he'd seen many of them that up close and personal. "Smart, too."

"Sounds like you've got a big helping of fatherly pride there."

He shrugged. "Just stating the truth. When I went back last night—"

"Back? You mean you went there before?"

"Yesterday morning. What's the matter, doesn't the Cowboy Creek gossip make it out here to the ranch?"

Cole snorted. "Sometimes I think it all gets reported in here. Jed always knows what's going on—though I'm not knocking him. I told you before, he's got a good heart. Now, what makes these kids of yours so smart?"

"When I picked them up out of their cribs again last night, they recognized me."

"How could you tell?"

"They smiled at me."

Cole snickered. "Man, newborns don't smile. They were only making faces at you because they were passing gas."

"No, they weren't."

Now the other man laughed out loud. "You think you have this new-daddy role figured out, don't you?" When

Tyler frowned, Cole raised both hands. "Calm down. I'm just pulling your leg, not picking on your kids."

The comment made him think of what he'd said to Shay about his father not supporting him. He hadn't intended to tell her that, but her easy assumption about his parents being as caring as Mo pushed him into it.

"There won't be anybody picking on Timothy once he gets bigger." He went on to tell Cole about the little boy's strength, Bree's patience, Jamie's playfulness… and a handful of other things. He hadn't realized he'd noted so much in just a couple of visits with the babies. After a while, he had to force himself to come to a stop. "Guess I'm boring you with all these stories."

"What are you talking about? I'll be trying to one-up you with stories of my own as soon as Tina has the baby. Speaking of which, you ought to think about staying around till then."

Suspicion made Tyler snap his response. "What for?"

"I already let the boss know I'll be taking time off once the baby arrives. We'll be shorthanded. That might be a good opportunity for you to slide right into a permanent spot here on the ranch. If you and Shay get a few things settled and you decide to stay, you'll need the work."

"Not going to happen, so don't go trying to play matchmaker." He'd already warned Jed about that, too.

"You ought to know." Cole shrugged. "Well, whatever happens, I'm taking the break. I might already be a daddy, but this is the first time I'll be around to see my son or daughter as a newborn. And this time, I'm not missing out on a thing."

When Cole walked away, Tyler stood deep in thought. Once he was gone from Cowboy Creek, there would be lots of new things happening with the babies, plenty of progress he'd never know about.

What did that matter? As Shay had reminded him, he didn't plan to get attached to the kids. He didn't intend to stick around. But while he was here, he had to stay close to her. It was plain from their truce last night that helping her with the babies was the key to earning her trust.

TYLER DROVE ALONG Canyon Road, the center of Cowboy Creek, feeling in a better frame of mind than he had in quite some time. After leaving the barn, he had run into Jed in the hotel hallway. The man claimed he'd been trying to hunt him down.

Between Jed and Cole, he didn't lack for people keeping an eye on him. But any irritation he might have felt fled once he'd finished talking with Jed.

Now, in the hospital parking lot, he tapped the hood of the car for good luck.

According to Jed, Shay had been given the okay from her doctor to bring the babies home. Upstairs, he found her in her room. Today her hair was smooth and flowing down her back. She wore a loose yellow top, jeans and a pair of running shoes. A small overnight bag sat on the floor beside the chair.

She looked at him in surprise. "What are you doing here?"

That seemed to be her standard question every time she saw him. Maybe his luck wasn't going to hold out, after all. "I'm taking you and the kids home."

"Grandma said she was picking us up."

"Jed told me Mo asked for help. Something about her women's circle and a big project they have to wrap up. She needed a stand-in, and Jed volunteered me. Are you ready to go?"

He could see the indecision in her face, the reluctance to accept his help at odds with the excitement at taking the kids home. So much for the truce he thought had been struck between them.

His luck held—her excitement won out.

"Yes, we're ready. Annabel's on her way with the wheelchair."

His mind flashed to the image of her being carried by stretcher to the ambulance. "Wheelchair? Is something wrong?"

"No. It's just a hospital rule."

"Oh." He forced a laugh. "Yeah, they have a lot of those around here."

She went to the cribs. He followed. The triplets were out of hospital wear today, too. They wore knitted caps and were wrapped in knitted baby blankets—blue for Timothy, green for Jamie and yellow for Bree.

"Three colors this time," he said.

"Yes. I didn't want to go with traditional pink and blue, anyway, and the reason for all the colors is, I didn't know how many of each we'd need."

"You didn't find out the sex of the babies beforehand?"

"No." She smiled. "I wanted to be surprised."

At least there had been *some* news she hadn't held back from him.

He glanced down again. "Well, you've got a pair, anyhow," he said, lifting Bree from the crib. He didn't care what Cole had told him—the baby's smile proved she recognized him. "She's all dressed up to match her mom."

"I didn't think of that," Shay said softly. "These were the first caps and blankets Grandma made, so I wanted them to be the first the babies used."

"Good idea. And since there are two of you dressed in yellow, obviously that color wins."

"I didn't think about that, either. But it's not a contest. We're all in this together."

Her words hung in the air for a long moment, and he wondered if she'd said them deliberately. *We* meant her and the babies. It didn't include him.

The silence stretched on as they stood there together, staring down at both boys in their cribs. Watching the babies sleep seemed to cast a spell over him, helping to push away some of his tension.

Annabel's cheerful arrival broke that spell. She had brought a couple of nurses with her to help carry the babies. A teenager wearing a volunteer badge said she had come along to assist with everything Shay had collected over the days she'd spent here. He noted she—or maybe a nurse—had put the three stuffed animals and the mug with the balloons on the windowsill.

He was still holding Bree. "I'm the official driver. I can carry Bree downstairs and take a bag of those gifts, too."

"I'm afraid not," Annabel said.

"Let me guess. You're not allowed to let me do that."

"You've got it." She gave him her small, sympathetic smile. "But as you're the chauffeur, you *can* go downstairs and bring your vehicle to the rear entrance of the building. You do have car seats for all three of the babies, don't you?"

"Of course."

To his satisfaction, this earned him a full smile from

every female in the room—except Bree, who had fallen asleep snuggled against his chest.

THEIR RELEASE FROM the hospital turned out to hold more surprises than Shay had expected.

The first had been seeing Tyler walk into her room and announce why he was there. She still wondered about Grandma's sudden absence. Yet, to her secret shame, she couldn't manage to suppress her little rush of happiness at knowing Tyler would help take the babies home.

She also couldn't keep from eyeing him when he wasn't looking. The sight of him standing in the bright sunshine streaming through the window beside her bed was enough to dazzle her. But it was the details that held her gaze. His dark hair gleamed, his belt buckle sparkled and his boots shone, as if he'd made a special effort to dress up this morning.

He had definitely made an impression with all three nurses and the teenage volunteer.

After he had left the room, the staff escorted her to the elevator for the trip downstairs.

"Was that your boyfriend?" the volunteer asked.

Keeping her gaze focused on her babies, she simply shook her head.

"He's a friend of Jed Garland's," Annabel announced. "Just came to give Shay and the triplets a ride home."

"Well," one of the other nurses said with a laugh, "any friend of Jed's is a friend of mine."

"Mine, too," the teenager said eagerly.

Listening to the women's conversation as they waited for the elevator, she fully expected them all to request Tyler's autograph when they saw him again downstairs. Or, in the case of the volunteer, to ask him for a date.

The little rush running through her now was a surge of pure jealousy, something she had no right or desire to feel. Resolutely, she pushed it down and determined to forget it. She didn't care who went after that cowboy.

The second surprise arrived when they reached the lobby, where a reporter from the local newspaper greeted them.

"Smile for the camera," she called.

Shay didn't need the encouragement. From the moment she had woken up that morning, she had been smiling from sheer happiness at the thought of taking her babies home.

Worry over how she would get rid of Tyler once they got there didn't make her quite as happy.

When he walked into the lobby, the reporter immediately latched on to him.

"No pictures," he said quickly. "I'm only the designated driver."

"Just one shot," she said, pretending to pout.

Shay frowned. He wouldn't believe in that act, would he? And what was wrong with the reporter, anyway? They had gone through school together, and in all those years she had never once seen the woman act this way.

Then again, the teenager and the two younger nurses were fawning over Tyler now, too, trying to convince him to take advantage of the photo opportunity. And yesterday, Patsy had giggled like a teenager.

Maybe his playboy charm was irresistible to any woman.

Maybe she shouldn't beat herself up for having fallen so hard and so fast. But she certainly wouldn't let herself fall again. She cared for him now as much as he had *ever* cared about her—which meant not one bit.

Her two attendant nurses put her sons into her arms, and she forgot about Tyler altogether...until he spoke again.

"I'm happy to hold a baby for the photo," he told the reporter, "as long as Shay agrees."

All five women swung their heads in her direction. Tyler stared at her, too. She stiffened, then forced herself to relax. With him acting so accommodating, she couldn't afford to look like the bad mom in this situation. Besides, after only a minute, the photo shoot would be over and they could be on their way.

All that mattered was her babies were going home.

The thought made her smile again.

Evidently taking that as an agreement, the reporter set them up for the photo. Shay sat in the wheelchair holding Timothy and Jamie. Tyler stood behind them with Bree in his arms.

After the reporter had gotten a number of shots, Annabel urged their group to the doors. "I know this is a big day for Cowboy Creek, but these babies need to get home for their next feeding."

"True," Tyler said. "Let's get them all strapped in."

And then came the final surprise of Shay's morning. When Annabel wheeled her out of the building, she saw the vehicle standing at the curb.

"You brought my car? And you had it washed?" she asked him in disbelief.

"Cleaned it myself," he said smugly. "Detailed it inside and out, too. I didn't think Annabel would approve of newborn babies in a dust-covered vehicle." The nurse laughed. "And after you've just had three babies, I sure don't want you having to climb up to get inside my pickup."

His concern about her children's health and her comfort touched her more than she could say. "Thanks," she murmured. But the word was drowned out by the awws and exclamations from all the women.

Tyler Buckham, playboy, strikes again.

They were halfway home before she remembered she didn't care.

HIS PLAN WAS WORKING.

Shay had been grateful he'd cleaned up her car for the ride home with the babies. Once they'd gotten to the house and upstairs to the babies' bedroom, she had seen the fully assembled cribs and turned away just a second too late to hide her suddenly teary eyes. Both reactions had to mean he'd taken at least one more step forward.

He looked around the room. "Mo said to wait for you to decide how you wanted everything set up."

"It's fine the way it is," she said faintly.

"What about this...whatever you'd call it? You surely don't want it here in the middle of the room."

"It's a changing table. Over there along the wall by the closet will work, please."

She had already prepared the bottles and was feeding Bree, sitting with her in a small pine rocker in one corner of the room.

Finished moving the table, he looked across at her and the baby. "Ladies first for a change, huh? That's a surprise."

"There have been a lot of surprises this morning." She paused, then continued, "When I went to get Timothy, Bree was already fussing."

"Is she done eating now? Let me put her in the crib." He took the baby from her. "Who do you want next?"

She hesitated, then said, "Timothy. He's been kicking at his blanket."

"He's not used to being second. And that's not like Bree to want to eat first. The other times I've been around, she's been willing to wait."

"I think she wanted to get ahead of the boys. I guess she's learning to assert her rights."

She put a slight emphasis on her final word. Again, an awkward silence fell, the way it had in her hospital room just before the nurses had shown up. What had she said then? *We're all in this together.* She and the babies.

Now he knew she'd deliberately aimed that comment at him. She had wanted to get the point across he was the odd man out. He handed Timothy to her and took a step back. "You might as well say outright what you're thinking."

Another silence fell. For a minute, he thought she was going to deny anything was bothering her. Then she took a deep breath and said flatly, "I don't like that you just showed up this morning without letting me know first."

"I told you, Jed asked me."

"But I didn't. I didn't know anything about it."

"I had no control over that."

"Even so, I don't like you thinking you can walk right into my hospital room and take over."

"I was trying to help out."

"The nurses were there."

"Forget that," he snapped. "This is all misunderstandings and things easily explained. Surface stuff. Why don't you go deep and tell me what's really bothering you?"

She cuddled Timothy close to her as if to shield the baby.

His heart thudded. She couldn't possibly feel she had to protect her kids from their own dad.

He blinked. When had he started thinking of himself in that role?

The deep breath he took didn't do much to steady his heart and his nerves.

No matter what he thought or what he did, he wouldn't win with Shay. She was determined to reject his good intentions. Clamping his jaws together, trying to hold back a response that wouldn't help matters at all, he simply stared at her.

She said nothing.

Despite his irritation, the steady creaking of the rockers on the wooden floor and the sight of her feeding Timothy began to calm him. Even Shay had seemed to relax a bit, her expression looking more serene.

He had a feeling this happy state wouldn't last long.

Before either of them could speak again, he heard the sound of the front door closing downstairs, then Mo's greeting. "Where are those great-grandbabies of mine?"

"In their bedroom," he called back.

Instantly, an expression of annoyance crossed Shay's face.

"What?" he demanded. "You think I'm taking over again, just because I answered Mo? Better that than have you yelling in Timothy's ear."

"It's not that," she said swiftly. "I don't think you should be here, around the babies. They'll just start getting used to you, and then you'll be gone."

"They're already used to me."

"No, they're not." She looked stricken but kept her

voice hushed, probably because she heard Mo's foot-steps in the hallway. "I want you to go."

He said nothing.

A few moments later, Mo entered the room and Shay said brightly, "Grandma's here now. She can help me."

"That I can't, I'm afraid," Mo said. "We've had an emergency call from the women's club, and they need me at the community center right away. I just stopped in for a moment to welcome you all home." She cupped her hand on Timothy's head and smoothed his hair. "There's my little love. *And* his brother and sister." She moved over to the cribs. "Tyler, you should unwrap Ja-mie's blanket a bit before he gets overheated."

He crossed the room.

"Grandma," Shay said almost plaintively, "can't you stay at least for a little while?"

"You'll be fine," Mo said in the same soothing tone she had used with Timothy. Obviously, she thought Shay was requesting assistance with the kids.

Tyler knew she wanted Mo to stay so he would leave.

"Where's Carol?" Shay asked. "I thought she was on the list to be here today."

"She was, but she called me earlier. Her own little one is down with the sniffles, and Carol doesn't want to bring any sickness around the babies. And rightly so." She smiled. "Isn't it fortunate we have Tyler here to help?"

Chapter Thirteen

Shay awoke with a start. She still sat in the rocking chair in one corner of the babies' room. Her first thoughts flew to the triplets, but from her seat she could see they all lay sleeping peacefully in their cribs.

Confused, she stared down at the afghan draped across her. She didn't remember covering herself with it. The last thing she recalled was Tyler taking Bree from her at the end of another round of feedings. She had watched him place the baby in her crib, then stop by each of the boys' cribs to check on them.

She had closed her eyes tightly to block out the sight of him and to stem back a sudden flow of tears.

And now here she was.

The room faced west, and sunlight slanting through the windows told her it was later in the afternoon. Horrified, she realized she had no idea exactly how long she had slept. Part of her day had disappeared. Evidently, so had Tyler.

She also realized she didn't know who was in the house with her.

After a quick check of the baby monitor on the dresser, she made her way downstairs. From the kitchen, the homey sounds of refrigerator and cupboard doors being opened and closed calmed her tension. Grandma was home again.

But it wasn't Grandma who stood at the stove holding a wooden spoon and stirring a small pot on one of the burners.

"Tyler! What are you still doing here?"

Muttering a curse, he started. The spoon fell to the floor. He picked it up and tossed it into the sink before turning to face her. "It would have been nice if you had coughed or something instead of sneaking up on me like that. Suppose I'd been holding one of the babies?"

He had a point. Flushing, she said, "Sorry. I just woke up. I'm not fully functional yet. And I don't know how I could have crashed like that. I didn't miss hearing any of the babies crying, did I?"

"Nope. I stayed upstairs for a while after you all went to sleep. And I haven't heard a peep out of that." With a fresh wooden spoon from the crock near the refrigerator, he gestured to the baby monitor on the counter.

"Thank goodness for that," she breathed. "But why are you still here? Where's Grandma?"

"She called a while ago and said she wouldn't be home again until later this afternoon."

She hadn't even heard the phone ring. "And you are…?" She pointed toward the stove, where steam rose from their biggest stockpot.

"I'm making supper."

"Grandma *asked* you to do that?"

"No. I volunteered. I make a mean baked ziti. I hope you're hungry." At that, her stomach gave a loud growl. He grinned. "Guess that answers my question."

"Of course I'm hungry. I haven't eaten since early this morning at the hospital."

"And the ziti won't be ready till tonight. Well, that won't do. How's tea and toast sound? That's about the only other thing I'm good for. Or eggs, if you'd rather have those."

"Toast sounds great," she admitted, "but you don't have to cook for me."

"I'm waiting for the water to boil, and you know what they say about a watched pot. Have a seat." He took the loaf of wheat bread from the bread box. "You have to eat to help keep up your strength to feed the babies. And you might as well conserve your energy while you have the chance."

Though it hadn't been a long walk from the kitchen to the bedroom, she was still feeling tender from her C-section. Her usual chair seemed to call to her. She took a seat at the table and, while Tyler's back was to her, watched each move he made. Filling the teakettle. Unerringly finding the plates in the cupboard near the sink and taking the butter dish from the top shelf of the refrigerator door. Adding pasta to the stockpot on the stove. He worked as if he were comfortable in the room, but as far as she knew, he'd never been in her kitchen... only in her bedrooms, both old and new.

After a few minutes, he carried her plate and tea mug to the table and set them down in front her. Then he went to the seat at the head of the table as if he had sat there many times before.

She stiffened.

"Don't worry," he said, "it's been washed more than once in hot, soapy water."

Only then did she notice the mug he had given her with the word *Mom* stenciled on it multiple times. Her eyes watered. She bit her lip to hide the smile that came so naturally to her. The smile she didn't want him to see. "How are you managing to find your way around our kitchen so easily?"

"Mo told me where to find the stew pot. The utensil drawer's easy to spot. Everything else is just common sense. Besides, I saw the dish cabinet when she gave me a cup of tea and a piece of cake."

"Today?"

"No, yesterday afternoon. I stopped by after I left the hospital."

Glancing down, she traced the handle of the mug with her finger. "When you finished assembling the cribs."

"Yeah."

Setting up the cribs had been his "least I could do" offer and part of the bargain that, technically, she hadn't yet agreed to when her pains had begun. Visiting her and the kids at the hospital, complete with gifts for them all, had gone beyond that least of his efforts. Bringing her and the babies home from the hospital, staying here with them, making tea and toast and ziti all were so far above *and* beyond what she had expected, she didn't know what to say.

She knew what she wanted to *believe*…but that wasn't somewhere her thoughts should go.

"Thank you for your help with the cribs and the bedroom," she said.

"No problem."

"Also for backing me up this afternoon. I don't know how I could have fallen so soundly asleep with three new babies to watch over." She paused, then added, "And I don't know what would have happened if you weren't here."

"If they had cried, you'd have woken up."

"I hope so."

"You would've. It's one of those mother's instincts you just haven't had to put to the test yet."

"Oh, really? And how would you know about that?" He smiled. His blatant attempt to make her feel better worked better than it should have. The smile did even more, sending a wave of pleasure through her. Again, she hesitated. Finally, she said, "You covered me with the afghan upstairs, too."

"Yeah. I didn't have the heart to wake you to see if you wanted it or not. You looked so tired."

She smiled wryly. "You're always good for a compliment, huh, Tyler?"

"I'm good for a lot of things." He reached out as if planning to touch her cheek. For a moment, he held his hand in the air. Then he pushed the plate a little closer to her. "Eat."

She took a bite from a half slice of toast. When she looked up again, he sat staring back solemnly, his gaze unblinking, his black lashes contrasting with his blue eyes. She drew in a breath and choked on a mouthful of crumbs. Covering her mouth with her arm, she coughed. And coughed.

He reached over and patted her back. "Now, that's the noise you should've made when you walked in here, instead of scaring me half to death."

She couldn't help but laugh.

His hand on her back stilled. His splayed fingertips grazed the back of her neck above her shirt, spreading warmth across her skin, sending hot shivers along her shoulders. Her mouth dried. She pressed her lips together, wanting to lick the taste of melted butter away but afraid he would take it as a tease. Resting his fingers against her neck might have been a move as innocent as when he cradled one of her babies' heads in his big hand.

Then he leaned closer, his eyes gleamed, and she knew her rationalizing hadn't come close to the truth. His touch was anything but innocent and his intentions even less so.

She wanted to protest. She had so many reasons to protest...

Before she could name one of them, he brushed his mouth against hers. All she could think of was how much time had passed since they had been together like this and just how much she had missed his kiss. Missed *him*.

Their relationship last summer hadn't given them much time with one another, but they hadn't needed time to learn what they each liked in a kiss. As he'd done back then, he started soft and easy and sweet but soon sent the heat level soaring. She could swear she heard a sizzle each time their lips parted and met again. Then she realized the sizzling was more than a feeling against her lips—it was a sound filling the air.

It was the sound of starch-filled water spattering on the stove top.

"I think something's burning," she murmured against his mouth.

"Darned straight," he said enthusiastically.

"No, I think something's burning on the stove."

He sat back, looked across the room and swore under his breath.

She wanted to pull him to her again, to lose herself in another kiss, to forget why she should keep her distance and why he wasn't the man for her. She didn't dare do any of that. Despite how his kisses made her feel, she couldn't give in. He didn't really care for her. He was just a playboy doing what he did best.

She sat back and grabbed her tea mug and stared down at it. The words inscribed on it danced before her eyes, reminding her just why she should protest if Tyler ever came close to her again.

IF ANYONE HAD ever told Tyler he would be having dinner with this family of five, three of them babies under the age of one week and one of them a woman he'd like under—

Whoa!

He reined in, bringing his thoughts to a bone-jolting halt. How could he think of the babies and…and want their mother, all in the same breath?

Looking down, he stabbed at his plateful of baked ziti, probably the best he'd ever made. It tasted as dry as dust to him. Fortunately, the other two adults in the room didn't think so.

"Tyler, you may cook for us anytime," Mo said, forking up another mouthful of pasta.

He smiled but didn't speak. There wouldn't be an *anytime*. That kiss this afternoon had shown him that. He needed to settle things with Shay. Tonight. After that, he wouldn't be back.

"This is delicious," Mo went on. "Isn't it, Shay?"

Beside him, she nodded but kept her gaze on her plate.

"It's my specialty. I'm not good at cooking much else," he admitted.

I'm good for a lot of things, he had said to Shay just before he lost the willpower to keep from kissing her.

Her gaze snapped up to meet his, then away. Was she remembering, too?

Both the statement and the kiss had been foolish moves on his part, considering the circumstances and his need to earn her trust. Worse, that foolishness had caused a major setback to his plan.

She had escaped from the kitchen while his back was turned and, for the rest of the afternoon, had stayed upstairs. After he'd gotten the ziti into the oven, he'd ventured up there, too, intending to apologize for his actions. He'd lost his nerve once he saw she sat holding one of the babies.

One of *their* babies...

Then Mo had arrived and he'd lost his chance, as well as his nerve. He had left the women together with the kids and come back downstairs to put the finishing touches on supper. Wanting to keep busy, to keep his mind occupied with something other than babies and kisses and Shay, he scrubbed the pots and utensils he had used to make supper. Then he needed another diversion. He had sat at the kitchen table with a copy of the local paper spread open in front of him.

At the supper table now, he smiled, thinking of the photo shoot at the hospital that morning and wondering when the picture would appear. He glanced across the room to the portable playpen Shay had set up in a quiet corner. He could see Timothy stirring. The kids would soon outgrow that small space, and the boy's strength could create a problem.

Tyler considered. He'd have to...

No, he would have to do nothing except give Shay enough money to buy a bigger playpen.

"I'll make corned beef and cabbage for you one

night," Mo said. "It doesn't call for as much work as your dish. Still, it's one of our favorites."

He could envision more nights around this table, with the babies a little bigger and sitting up in high chairs, spreading mashed-up peas on the trays with their fingers. A good thing the adults and kids were evenly matched.

Once he was gone, the adults would be outnumbered.

He couldn't control that. But he could keep Mo—and Shay—from making plans around him. "I doubt I'll be here for too many more nights."

Again, Shay's gaze snapped to his, then moved away.

Mo sent him an unreadable half smile.

Timothy let out a little wail. Shay pushed back her chair and went to the playpen.

He had no clue what Mo's expression meant. He didn't care to know. Not wanting to encourage her and grateful for the excuse to look away, he glanced over at the babies. "Sounds like that boy's lungs are getting stronger by the day. You're going to have yourselves a time when they all start yelling like that at once."

"We are, indeed," Mo agreed.

Shay lifted Timothy from the playpen. "I'll take him upstairs. He likes me to rock him while he eats."

He watched her cross the room and walk through the doorway. He wondered whether she had left just to get some distance from him. The thought shouldn't have bothered him. But it did.

He looked back to find Mo staring at him from across the table. She smiled, a full smile this time. "You've been wonderful these past few days, Tyler, helping with the cribs and then bringing the babies home with Shay.

I don't know what we'd have done without you today, too. I'm grateful to have your help again tomorrow."

"Tomorrow? I don't—"

She leaned forward and said in an urgent whisper, "Let's turn off that baby monitor for a moment, shall we? It picks up sound from both directions, and I'd just as soon keep this conversation between us."

Nodding, he rose. What was this about? A prickle of unease made his shoulders stiffen. Once he had turned off the monitor, he went back to his seat.

"You've been very giving of your time," Mo said quickly, "and I would never ask this of you if I weren't in a bind. But that's exactly it, you see. I've run into some trouble. Our helper scheduled for tomorrow has had to cancel, too. And just the hour or so upstairs with Shay and the babies this afternoon wore me out." She sighed. "Though I would never in a million years say this to Shay, I'm forced to admit it to you. Tyler, three babies are just too much for me to handle."

I need your help.

She didn't have to say it. He could see it in her eyes.

Now a hint of mistrust blended with his unease. The woman looked spry enough to him. She sure seemed to have enough get-up-and-go to roam all over town. It sounded like she all but ran the women's club and the knitting circle and a bunch of other groups. But despite her apparent energy and her clear green eyes, as he had already noted, her hair was as snow white as Jed's. No doubt she came somewhere close to the man's seventy-something years.

He also had noticed how much those green eyes were like Shay's.

Unlike her granddaughter lately, Mo held his gaze. He couldn't have looked away if his life depended on it.

And he wouldn't turn her down.

It felt good to finally have *someone* willing to trust and depend on him.

Chapter Fourteen

Finished settling Timothy in his crib, Tyler turned to watch Shay. She stood at the changing table closing the snaps on Jamie's pajamas, just as he had done a minute ago with Timothy. "I'm getting pretty good at this baby-changing business, don't you think?"

She threw him a glance. "*Pajama* changing, you mean. You don't get credit for the full job unless you've changed the diaper, too."

"Well, that's where I have to draw the line. But my tucking skills aren't bad, either. Here, give Jamie to me. I'll put him back in his crib."

He had given in to Mo's request for more help. Since his return this morning, he and Shay had tiptoed around each other—and not solely because they didn't want to wake the kids.

She had been careful to keep out of his reach ever since he'd kissed her yesterday. Obviously, she regretted that kiss as much as he did. There was nothing he could do about his actions except apologize. The opportunity for that conversation had never arisen, and he felt reluctant to bring it up now.

When he walked up to her, she nearly shied away. Just as obviously, she was still being careful, choosing not to get too close to him again. She had the right idea. They seemed to have reinstated the truce that had been broken after they'd brought the babies home from the hospital. He didn't want to say anything to damage that again.

He lifted Jamie, holding the baby's head the way the nurse had taught him. "Doc Grayden's going to be impressed when he sees this big guy. He's put on weight since we brought him home."

"They all have."

Rooting for the underdog, he had already starting encouraging the smaller of the two boys to be more active. "He's getting to be as strong as Timothy already, too. Watch this." Carefully, he touched his little finger to Jamie's fist. The baby spread his tiny fingers, then latched them around Tyler's pinky. "That's the way, buddy," he murmured. Grinning, he told Shay, "He did that yesterday for the first time. Now whenever I touch his fist, he grabs on. He thinks it's a game."

"Does he?"

"Sure he does." And every time those little fingers wrapped around his, Tyler felt his chest constrict. "I bet he'll be great with a lasso."

"I doubt he'll ever have his hands on one."

"Why not? This is cowboy country. Ropin' needs to be on every kid's list of skills."

"No, it doesn't. Not if he doesn't plan to be a cowboy. And he won't. Neither will Timothy."

Frowning, Tyler returned Jamie to his crib. After a deep breath, he turned to face Shay again. "The babies aren't a week old yet. How can you know what they'll want to be when they grow up?"

"I'm their mom."

"That's a heck of a reason. And a crazy one. You can't plan your kids' entire lives when they're still in the cradle." Too bad nobody had told his parents that. "But I guess some people don't care. You and my folks would get along just fine."

"They don't like having a rodeo cowboy for a son?" she asked coolly.

"I think sometimes they don't like having a son at all. But no, they don't like the fact I'm a cowboy."

"Because they probably want more for you than that."

"Why do I need more?" Her words and expression made something click in his mind. "The afternoon we came back here with your shower gifts, you told me you appreciated the reminder I was *only* a rodeo cowboy. What did that mean?"

"Nothing. That's what you are, isn't it?"

"Yeah. But why did you need the reminder?"

She shrugged. "No reason."

He didn't buy that answer for a minute. She had a reason, all right, and though he was *only* a rodeo cowboy, not a rocket scientist, he had figured it out. "You're not going to let the kids make up their own minds. You're going to keep them from becoming wranglers because *I'm* one, aren't you?"

"Don't flatter yourself."

He clenched his jaw. Clearly, she wasn't any more impressed than his parents were by his choice of career. Like them, she felt cowboys didn't amount to much.

SHAY WATCHED ANXIOUSLY as Dr. Grayden went to each crib in turn, checking the triplets' eyes and ears and testing their reflexes. When he touched Jamie's hand, she couldn't help but smile as she recalled Tyler grinning with pleasure over Jamie clutching his finger. Over Jamie playing their game.

At the thought of the rest of that conversation, her smile slid away.

Once, her dad's broken promises had broken her heart. Tyler's refusal even to make promises hurt so much more. She would cope—she would always survive, even without him. But *how* could she have fallen for a rodeo cowboy just like her dad?

Dr. Grayden tucked his wire-rimmed glasses into his breast pocket and turned to her. "I'd say they're thriving, Shay. Amazing what a steady diet and a little love can do, isn't it?"

"A lot of love, Doctor," she corrected. "Grandma and I and...well, the two of us just can't get enough of them."

"That's good. Sometimes with multiple births, a new mother is too tired to interact with her babies except during feedings. Physical contact is critical, especially in these early days."

"No problems there." Even Tyler had done his fair share of holding the babies. Connecting to the babies. But not for much longer. She sighed.

"Something worrying you?"

She started, not realizing he had heard her sigh. She shrugged. "I have to admit to being tired."

He patted her arm. "That's almost a given with one baby. With three it's impossible to avoid. I gather you're having no trouble sleeping when you have the opportunity?"

"Oh, no," she assured him as they left the bedroom. "I nap every chance I get." Guiltily, she thought of waking up in the rocking chair. She had been truthful with

Tyler—she didn't know what she would have done if he hadn't been there.

Downstairs, Dr. Grayden repeated the results of the babies' checkup for the benefit of Grandma and Layne. Once he had left, Grandma gestured to the teapot on the coffee table.

"A cup for you, Shay?"

She nodded and reached to take her Mom mug from the tray. Grandma must have noticed that she had started to use it. The mug had already become her favorite... because she *was* a mom now, multiple times over, and not because Tyler had been the one to give it to her.

After Grandma had poured the tea, she said, "I think I'll just go up and check on my great-grands."

Shay and Layne looked at the baby monitor on the end table beside the couch, then exchanged smiles.

As they watched Grandma move out of sight up the stairs, Shay murmured, "She hasn't had as much time as she'd like with the babies. She's been so busy, even more than normal." She frowned. After a moment, she realized Layne hadn't responded. She looked over to find her friend eyeing her.

"And...?" Layne asked.

"And what?"

Layne rolled her eyes. "Mo might be busy, but I hear you're not all on your own with the babies. She tells me Tyler was here all day yesterday, and today, too, until he left just a while ago. What's up?"

"I don't know. It's very odd. Every person on our list of mother's helpers has let us down."

"That's not what I mean, and you know it."

Shay pulled the afghan from the back of the couch and settled it in her lap as if it could shield her from

Layne's question and from thoughts she didn't want to have. The action again made her recall waking up in the rocking chair to find Tyler had draped an afghan over her. He looked after her as well as he did the babies.

When Grandma had arrived home this afternoon, followed a few minutes later by Layne, Tyler had announced he was off to run errands. He hadn't been gone five minutes when she found herself missing him. Since yesterday, she hadn't been able to get through more than ten minutes at a stretch without thinking about their kiss.

Flushing, she settled back against the couch. "I don't know what's up," she admitted. "I'm surprised Tyler didn't stay to find out the results of the checkups. He takes as good care of the babies as I do. Better, even. He's a natural, Layne."

"That's great. So why do you look like you're about to lose your best friend?"

No, she was about to lose something much more than that. "Whether he's got the knack or not, he's still not ready to be a daddy."

"Then make him ready."

She shook her head. "I can't. Besides, I don't want him around the babies."

"Yeah," Layne said drily, "I can see that, all right."

Again, Shay flushed. Layne had hit on the one thing that had bothered her since Tyler had first come to the hospital. She *did* want him around the babies—permanently. Except…how did that old saying go?

If wishes were horses, beggars would ride.

She wasn't about to beg him to stay. Or to accept handouts he offered only because he felt pressured into giving them. She couldn't let a few tender moments with the kids and a heart-stoppingly hot kiss make her give in. "He's still a cowboy," she said bitterly.

"And he'll probably always be a cowboy," Layne said in a soft tone, "just like nine-tenths of the men in Cowboy Creek. If you're holding out for someone who *doesn't* wear boots and a Stetson to work, you may be waiting a very long time."

"Stop. You know what I mean." She and Layne had long ago shared the stories of their childhoods. "I won't get involved with a cowboy."

Layne laughed. "Too late for that, girlfriend. Once you're sharing children, you're already as involved as you can get." She sobered. "Look, I know it was rough for you, not having your dad around and, most of the time, not your mom, either. But there are worse things than absentee parents."

Yes, like falling for a man she couldn't trust.

"You're right," she said. Layne and Cole had grown up with parents who were there physically but didn't support them in any way. Tyler seemed to think his parents were made from the same mold. She couldn't see his situation from that perspective. To her, what he had said made it clear his mom and dad cared about his future. What more could a child ask of a parent?

Seeing how Tyler cared for her and the babies, what more could she ask of him?

AFTER HIS TENSE conversation with Shay, Tyler had been glad when Mo and Layne showed up at the house within minutes of each other. It gave him the excuse he needed to walk away. He might only be a rodeo cowboy, but he had smarts enough to know where he wasn't wanted.

And when a rodeo cowboy felt his presence wasn't welcome, he…

…went shopping?

Swallowing a laugh, he shoved the paper sack under his arm. The boys at the ranch in Texas had better not hear about this.

He rang Shay's doorbell, feeling eager to get back inside the house. In this short time away from the kids, he had missed them.

Suddenly, he realized his eagerness came from more than just *missing* the babies. Now that he had seen and held them, changed their pajamas and watched them smile, he had grown to care about them. His obligations had become much more personal.

These were his kids. He needed to provide for them.

As for Shay…well, she'd been right all along. Despite the family they'd begun, he wasn't the man for her.

And considering the way she felt about his being a cowboy, she sure wasn't the woman for him.

The door opened. Shay stood looking up at him, one hand gripping the door. The lowering sun made her squint. The light turned her eyes into sparkling emeralds. Her long hair had fallen forward over her shoulders and trailed down the front of her shirt, the blond strands looking like pure gold in the light.

He cleared his throat. "How are the babies doing?"

"They're still sleeping."

"All good, then." Her face was pale with faint shadows below her eyes. Before he could think twice about it, he raised his hand to her face and traced his thumb lightly along her cheekbone. "Did you get any rest?"

She shook her head. Her hair brushed the back of his hand. They weren't meant for each other, and yet he couldn't keep from running his fingers down the long strands of her hair. He settled his hand at her waist. She had filled out since last summer, and the knowledge that her lusher curves and thicker waist had come from carrying his babies filled him with a need he couldn't name or describe or resist.

He slid his hand around to press it against her back and tilted his head closer to hers. For the life of him, he couldn't recall why he'd been irritated when he had left here or why he'd taken so long to come back. For his pride's sake, he only hoped she wanted to kiss him as much as he wanted to kiss her.

To his undying relief, she tilted her chin up, willing, but waiting for him to make his move. A growl rose inside his chest, like the building roar of a lion preparing to defend his jungle.

He didn't want to raise any defenses with Shay— he wanted her against him, willing and warm and his.

When Tyler tightened his arm around her waist, Shay nearly melted into him. As always, his mouth was sure on hers. This time, his kiss was immediately hot and hungry, as if he were too impatient to give her the slow and easy buildup she had learned to love.

She discovered jumping straight to hot and hungry could satisfy her as well.

She curled her fingers in the fabric of his shirt and pulled him closer. When he raised his hand to the back of her head to hold her steady, to deepen his kiss, she wrapped her arms around him. The crackle of paper and the sudden stab of a hard protrusion into her milk-swollen breast—from well above his waistline—made her grunt in surprise.

He raised his head and stared down at her. "What's wrong?"

"I...uh...think you just poked me...with something." She laughed uncontrollably and covered her mouth with one hand. With the other, she pointed to the sack he held under his arm.

"Oh. Sorry." He smiled. "It's something for the kids. But I didn't plan on giving it to you this way."

Her thought in response to *that* statement made her cheeks burn.

Her feelings for him flared just as hot, her response to his kiss overwhelming. Out-of-whack hormones, that's what she had to blame, along with lack of sleep and tension over trying to take care of three newborns at once. She *couldn't* feel anything for Tyler.

And still, she did.

As hard as she had fought to deny the truth to herself, she had to accept it now. The day they had met, she had done more than fall for him. She had given him her heart.

Now, she couldn't go back into the house and face Grandma, not with her face still flushed and her pulse still pounding. Quickly slipping through the doorway past Tyler, she crossed to the wooden porch swing and sank onto it.

He followed, as she had dreaded but known he would. He couldn't do what he did best from a distance.

After taking a seat beside her, he plopped the sack into her lap.

She looked down. "You already bought gifts for the kids—the stuffed animals."

"And now I bought them something else. I'm entitled." She said nothing, and a beat later, he added quickly, "After all, I've been one of the best babysitters they've ever had."

"The *only* babysitter, you mean."

"Even more reason for me to spoil them." He gestured to the sack. "Go ahead, open it."

She unrolled the top and reached inside the sack. Her fingers touched something soft and padded. She pulled out a stuffed terry-cloth pony with a mane made of woolen strands. Then she pulled out its twin and finally their triplet. Each wore a ribbon around its neck—blue, green or yellow, just like the blankets and caps her babies had worn home from the hospital.

She didn't know whether to laugh or cry. All his gifts were heartfelt and precious. And they weren't enough.

Her heart ached, but looking at the silly smiles on the ponies' faces finally brought a small smile to her lips, too. "Thank you. The babies will love them."

"There's more," he said.

"Oh." She reached into the sack again and pulled out a handful of tiny garments on plastic hangers—the source of the surprising stab that had interrupted their kiss. The hangers held one-piece pajamas patterned with horses. A multipack of bibs sported horseshoes and saddles.

She couldn't miss the message.

One way or another, Tyler was determined to have their babies grow up to be cowboys.

SHORTLY AFTER HIS greeting to Shay on the front porch, Tyler sat sharing yet another meal with her and Mo.

The conversation when he'd come back home…come back *here*…had been all he could have asked for. Shay hadn't rejected him when he had taken her into his arms. Heck, that kiss might have gone on for quite some time if the sack he'd held hadn't gotten in the way.

Mo looked across the table, beaming at him. "Those are lovely gifts you brought for the babies, Tyler."

He laughed, shrugging. Why he'd gone into the department store and wandered to the children's section, he still didn't know. "Kind of a coals to Newcastle gift, bringing new clothes into a house already filled with them. But I saw them on the hangers and that was that."

"Ah, but infants need more clothing than most children."

He frowned, puzzled. "I'd have said they would hardly need anything but diapers and an outfit or two."

"They grow so quickly," Shay explained. It was the first time she had spoken since they'd sat down to supper.

"That they do," Mo agreed. "Sometimes they barely have the chance to wear an outfit before they've outgrown it."

"But not bibs," he said quickly.

"No, not bibs." Mo laughed, and even Shay smiled.

To his satisfaction, she had seemed to like the gifts he'd brought. Of course, a new mom would probably be overjoyed by anything given to her babies. Still, he told himself she especially liked his gifts. *And* his kiss. To his surprise, he found the knowledge of each brought him equal pleasure.

Now, her brow wrinkled in a frown, Shay stared down at her serving of the chicken casserole that had been delivered by a friend. "I don't understand this, Grandma," she said, sounding bewildered. "The women of Cowboy Creek are there for each other, always. And you and I have never hesitated to help anyone out. All our friends who signed up to bring food are delivering as promised. But we had a full roster of assistants, and not one of them has shown up."

He didn't get it, either, but he knew better than to say so. For sure, he realized the wisdom of keeping quiet about his agreement with Mo.

"They've had their reasons, lass."

"Well, yes. Sickness and toothaches, I can understand. But a haircut and a manicure?"

"Those seemed rather flimsy reasons, to be sure," Mo agreed. While her granddaughter's attention was still diverted, she shot Tyler a glance, then quickly looked away again.

Suspicion landed like a punch to his gut. Shay was right. Some of those women were bailing out with poor excuses. Did Mo have a hand in that? Had she arranged to have the women skip their assignments? But with Mo too busy to help, why would she leave a brand-new mom like Shay on her own with three babies?

Because…because Shay hadn't been alone. She'd had him here.

As if Mo had read his mind, she said, "We've been very fortunate that Tyler could help out."

He narrowed his eyes. He sensed strings being pulled here and felt sure she wasn't working alone. Jed Garland had his hands in this, too. He was certain of it.

Was that the matchmakers' plan—to give him and Shay time alone? If so, their plan had succeeded. And was that why Jed had claimed he would be busy at the wedding reception the other day—the old man had deliberately left him at loose ends, hoping to drive him to the Big Dipper and Shay? That had worked, too.

He'd been played.

He'd also been given time to play.

But much as he liked the idea of another kiss, a cuddle and the hope of something more, getting even closer to Shay wasn't a smart idea. Not when he'd be leaving again...soon.

Judging by her stiff expression, she seemed to be thinking along the same lines. "We...we can't keep relying on Tyler," she told Mo.

I can't rely on Tyler. That's what she meant.

He had walked away from her once and, kisses aside, it seemed she planned to hold that action against him forever.

Chapter Fifteen

From the back booth of SugarPie's, his favorite seat, Jed Garland could watch everything that went on in the sandwich shop. He could even get a peek through a doorway into the adjacent bakery. Both shops were quiet now, though. At this hour of the morning, too early even for the townsfolk to be headed to work, no one had stopped in yet to have breakfast or to pick up some of Sugar's famous sweet rolls.

He reached for the plateful of them she had just set in front of him.

"Is Mo stopping in?" she asked.

He swallowed a smile. Sugar Conway was appropriately named, all right. Her sugar-wouldn't-melt-in-my-mouth Southern accent might deceive those who didn't know her. But he'd watched her eject a rambunctious group of teens from the shop without lifting a finger. No, her sweet tone didn't fool him.

"You know darned well Mo's meeting us here this morning," he said. "I gather that's the reason I'm getting your special attention. You're as eager as I am to find out what's going on with Shay."

Laughing, she wedged herself into the seat across from him. "Jed, *you* know darned well you get the royal treatment every time you walk in. And yes, I want to hear what's going on. Tongues have been wagging in here and all over town."

"That's only natural for folks in Cowboy Creek. But Mo and I between us have managed to keep everyone away from the house." He filled her in on the latest developments with the new mom and her brood...and their daddy. "We're very pleased with the way Tyler's managing to take care of the babies."

"That does sound promising. Besides, he wouldn't hang around if he didn't have an interest."

"In the babies *or* in their mama," he agreed. "We just need to find out which one's the driving force." He glanced past her. "And here's Mo now. Let's hope she's got an answer."

Mo took a seat in the booth beside him. Sugar reached across the table with the carafe and poured her a mug of coffee.

"Thanks, Sugar."

"It'll cost you," the other woman said with a grin. "Let's have the news."

Even he couldn't wait to hear. "Which one has Tyler got his eye on?"

"Both," she said promptly. "That's my best guess. Yesterday afternoon Jim Grayden stopped in to check on his patients. Tyler left for a while, then came home with an armload of gifts for the babies."

"And for Shay?" he asked.

"I'm thinking he gave her something, too." She smiled. "Just after he returned, they spent some time out on the front porch. When they walked into the kitchen, her hair was mussed and she looked apprehensive, as though afraid I would guess what the two of them had been up to."

"Too bad you don't know for sure," Sugar said.

"Who says I don't?" Mo grinned wickedly. "I peeked into the living room and saw them together at the front door. As in, lips locked together."

"So everything's going according to plan," Sugar said complacently.

"Well…" Mo shifted her coffee mug in a circle on the tabletop.

"Out with it, woman," Jed demanded. "The news sounds promising. But what's got you on the fence?"

"I don't quite know. It's hard to put my finger on it, but something's still not right between them."

"Even after their kissing in broad daylight?"

"Yes. And we've had a major upset to our plans this morning, as well. Tyler called just as I was leaving home and said he won't be by today."

"What?" He frowned. "The boy left the hotel bright and early this morning, as usual."

"Well, he didn't come our way."

"Hmm." He brooded for a minute. "I think maybe those two need a break from the babies. Some time on their own to talk, and to get up to whatever they want to get up to."

"Oh, that will never work," Mo protested. "Shay won't leave her little ones, not for a good while."

"She won't have to if you volunteer to bring them out to the ranch with her this afternoon. Tell her Tina and the other girls want to see the babies. Also, tell her I need to see her about her hours at the Hitching Post. She can hardly say no to either of those, now can she?"

"But what about Tyler?"

"Don't worry. I'll take care of him."

AT FIRST, SHAY had balked about taking the babies out to Garland Ranch. On their visit, they could run into Tyler. Or, worse, they might not.

"Isn't it too soon for the babies to be out?"

"They've already been exposed to plenty of hospital staff and visitors," Grandma had said. "And we're only planning to see Jed and the girls while we're out there."

Jed and his granddaughters…and not the babies' daddy?

The question made her determined to turn down the trip to the Hitching Post.

The message Grandma passed along that Jed wanted to see her had made her change her mind. In the dark hours of the night, alone in her bedroom between feedings, she would—and did—allow herself to think about Tyler. At any other time, her thoughts had to focus on taking care of her babies. Extra hours at the Hitching Post would go a long way toward helping with that.

Now, in the sitting room of the hotel, she watched Tina and Jane and Andi ooh and aah over the babies. She couldn't help but smile. At the same time, her spirits sank lower than they had when she and Grandma and the triplets had arrived. As she had feared, Tyler had been nowhere to be found.

Maybe he had left town already. Maybe that was why he had called to say he wouldn't be at the house—he was on his way out of Cowboy Creek.

He had hung up after delivering his message to Grandma, not even asking to speak with her. She didn't care. So then why, ever since that phone call, did it feel as though her heart had broken?

So much for not thinking about the man.

Tina looked up from cuddling Bree. "Robbie was so disappointed he couldn't be here. Once Grandpa Jed told him the babies were coming for a visit, he didn't want to go to school this morning."

"Neither did Rachel," Jane said. "And I heard about it all the way to the bus stop."

Everyone laughed. Even Shay managed a genuine smile. Pete's young daughter never hesitated to share her thoughts. "Robbie will have a baby brother or sister to keep him company soon."

"That doesn't matter," Tina said. "He still wants to see the triple kids, as he calls them."

Shay laughed. "Then I'll plan to bring the babies out here again soon. Or you all can come visit us at home." At home, where she and the babies and Grandma would get along just fine without...their absent helper.

"I'm not sure where you'll find the time to spend at the house, lass," Grandma said. "Not if Jed's planning to give you more hours."

"And I hope he is," she admitted.

"I'm pretty sure he is," Tina said with a smile. As the bookkeeper, she would probably know. "But don't let him hear I spoiled the surprise."

"I won't." Shay didn't want to spend time away from the babies. She didn't want more hours, but she needed them. As a bonus, staying busy would help keep her mind off her worries. It would help remind her—as if she could forget—that she was now a parent and had obligations...

Which was just the way Tyler felt.

How could she have been so upset with him about that?

The sudden sound of boot heels and deep voices from the hallway made her pulse spike. The sight of Tyler standing beside Jed in the hotel's wide sitting room doorway set off a fluttering in her chest.

His gaze met hers, then jumped to the babies. She couldn't fault him for that at all. She wouldn't have had it any other way.

"Abuelo, look who's here." Tina rose and crossed the room to show off Bree.

"Well, let me get my hands on that little girl." Jed took the baby from her. "She's a cute one, isn't she, Tyler?"

He smiled and nodded. "Gonna be a heartbreaker someday."

Just like her daddy.

Tyler reached over to adjust Bree's knitted cap, then stood smiling down at her. His half smile and rapt expression made Shay's eyes sting with tears. He'd become so good at handling the kids in such a short time. Even more, he cared about them. She could see that plainly, even if no one else could. Even if he wouldn't admit it to her.

He cared for his babies, that's what counted most.

And she cared for him. She loved him and always had. That had to count for something, too. She had to talk to him, to find the courage to tell him how she felt. And most of all, to make sure he would be there for their babies.

HALFWAY DOWN THE hall to the Hitching Post's kitchen, Shay reached Jed's den, where Tina had told her to meet him.

She stepped into the room and stopped short. No Jed. Instead, Tyler sat on the couch along one wall, his legs stretched out in front of him, boots crossed at the ankles, giving every appearance he had settled in. If only she could convince him to feel that way about Cowboy Creek.

"I'm supposed to meet Jed here," she said.

"So am I. Have a seat." He began to rise.

"Don't get up." When she took one of the visitor's chairs by the desk, he sank back into his seat. She had wanted to speak to him privately, but not here, not now. When Jed walked in, she would need a clear head to discuss her job at the Hitching Post. But if Tyler did plan to leave town at any moment, this might be the only chance she had to talk with him.

She rested her hands on the arms of the chair and shot a glance in his direction.

"The babies look fine this morning," he said stiffly.

"They *are* fine."

"Is Timothy still ruling the roost at mealtime?"

"He is. But Bree beat Jamie to her bottle this morning." At the memory, she couldn't help but smile.

He did, too, a small, almost wistful smile. "Wish I'd been there—"

"You could have been," she said quietly. "You could be there often, if you wanted to." He ran his hand down his arm, smoothing his shirtsleeve. Or was he literally brushing away her words?

Uneasiness ran through her. She took a deep breath and reminded herself she had found the courage to do this. "Tyler, maybe we went about everything out of order, with me getting pregnant before we had the chance to have a real relationship. But I... You have to know how much I care about you. I care about your relationship with the kids, and I see how much you care about them, too. We can make sure your relationship with *them* goes the right way. If you'll stay in Cowboy Creek."

Now he rose from the couch. Though he stood a few feet away, his height and broad shoulders still managed to give the impression he towered over her. She didn't fear him. Just the opposite. Heat flushed her cheeks and flooded her body, and she knew her appeal to him to stay in town came equally from concern for her babies—*their* babies—and wishes for her own future happiness.

He stood shaking his head. "That's not going to work, Shay. I know it. And you know it. We don't agree on a single thing, especially when it comes to the kids."

"What do you mean? We agree on lots of things—"

"Not the ones that matter."

Now her seated position made her feel she was losing ground. She stood to face him. "I told you, my dad followed the rodeo, too, and—"

"And that's exactly what I'm talking about. We don't agree on the work I do. We don't even agree on the gifts I bring home...bring to the kids. Bibs and pajamas. How could I go wrong with those? But somehow, they're not good enough for you."

"Bibs and pajamas with horses and saddles on them. They were just your way of trying to get your point across." Her eyes stung with angry tears. "Maybe I'm wrong about being able to make your relationship with the babies work. You're not thinking about them at all."

"I am, probably more than you are. You're the one

pulling strings already, when they haven't even cut their first teeth."

"How is that any different from what you're doing? The last I heard, you've got your plans for them all mapped out, too."

"No. I was showing you an alternative. I'm trying to give the kids options."

She gasped. "And don't you think that's what I want?"

"I think you're controlling their futures—"

"I'm not." She stopped and took a deep, steadying breath. Arguing like this would only help to prove Tyler's claim that they couldn't agree on anything. "You're just seeing me the way you are because of how your father treated you."

"And you're not holding what I do for a living against me, for the same reason? I'm a cowboy. That doesn't mean I'm just like your dad." He shoved his hands into his back pockets. "It doesn't matter. I'm not staying. That's what I told you from the beginning, and I never said anything otherwise. As it is, I shouldn't have stayed this long. You've made it plain you don't trust me, but I'm telling you something you can take to the bank— literally. Not a promise. Fact. I'll be sending you cash to help support the kids."

The words hit like a knife piercing her heart.

"I don't want your charity," she snapped.

"It's not a handout. It's—"

"I know. It's your *obligation*. Money. Financial help. And you, at a distance." Her frustrated sigh bordered on a sob. "How can you walk away from our babies, especially after all the time you've spent with them? They've bonded with *you* as strongly as they have with me."

He said nothing.

She wanted him here, being a daddy to her children. He wanted to negotiate a deal and then write the babies off as a business expense.

She took another deep breath and let it out slowly. "Nothing I've said—or can say—will change your mind?"

"No."

The unyielding response left her speechless from stunned surprise and a flash of rage. The reaction gave her a beat of time to raise her defenses, to realize she was determined to win this battle…even if she'd already been defeated in the war.

She would not let him see her break. She raised her chin. "It's just as well, then," she said firmly. "If you're not prepared to stay for the long haul, you might as well leave town."

Chapter Sixteen

When a resounding knock thumped against his door, Tyler started. He stared suspiciously across the hotel room. He had left Shay downstairs in Jed's den only a short while ago. She wouldn't have had time to reconsider anything he'd said. And surely, she wouldn't have told Jed about their conversation.

The knock came again.

"It's open," he called.

The door swung wide. Cole stepped into the room and shut the door quietly behind him. "Hey, buddy, what's going on? Tina tells me you're all of a sudden set on leaving."

"Nothing sudden about it. I've been planning to go for days now. I told her I'd be checking out this afternoon. It's about time I got back home."

Home. Where there would be no babies, no Shay. And now, not even a job for him to go back to.

Cole started across the room.

"Don't get comfortable." He knew his buddy well. Give the man a minute and he'd talk for an hour or more. Tyler took his duffel bag from the closet and tossed it onto the bed. "I'm leaving as soon as I've packed."

Ignoring him, Cole dropped into one of the armchairs by the window. "So I hear. Just one question. Have you lost your mind?"

Tyler stiffened. "What does that mean?"

"You know what it means, man. You're a brand-new daddy. And you're walking away from your kids? From your family?"

"Stop right there. We're not a family."

Cole shrugged. "Okay, maybe not at the moment. But you'll never have a chance of becoming one if you're nowhere in sight."

And you, at a distance.

Shay had called that right. He was planning to put miles between him and Cowboy Creek. "What are you, an advice columnist now?" He opened the dresser drawer and scooped up a handful of T-shirts. "You've been hanging around these matchmakers too long."

"Hanging around, heck." The other man grinned. "I'm a walking, talking advertisement for their services."

Tyler dropped the shirts into his bag. "I'm glad it worked out well for you. I'm not in the market."

"You might live to regret that."

"But I'll live."

"What kind of life, though?"

Tyler laughed shortly. "And now you're a shrink, asking me to contemplate the meaning of existence? Give it up, Cole. Not all of us take to being a dad the way you have."

"That'll come with a little practice. Believe me, I didn't know if I could handle it at first, either. You haven't been with the kids long enough to know what kind of dad you'll make."

"I'm not talking about *learning* the ropes. I meant not all of us *want* to be roped and tied."

That stopped the other man—for about two seconds. "Funny, I used to think exactly that myself. Sorry to hear you saying it, too. And that's your final word?"

Nothing I've said—or can say—will change your mind?

"That's it."

Cole sighed. "So be it. Then here's my final piece of advice, no charge. I know you well enough to realize why you're running. I also know from my experience it's something you need to work through on your own. But don't wait too long, or you might miss out." He crossed the room, and they shook hands. "The Hitching Post will have a room waiting when you change your mind."

"I won't."

"Suit yourself. But in any case, the room will be here. Don't be a stranger. Like it or not, the Garlands consider you family."

They've bonded with you *as strongly as they have with me.*

TYLER HAD BARELY made it to the bed again with a handful of socks when another knock came to the door. This one sounded soft, almost tentative. His heart jumped to his throat.

He crossed the room and opened the door. Shay's grandma stood in the hallway. He swallowed hard and stepped back. "Would you like to come in?"

"That *is* why I'm paying you a visit, love. One of the reasons, at any rate." Like Cole, she claimed a seat by the window.

This time, he followed and took the armchair opposite. He could be as rude and blunt as he liked with Cole, but Grandma Mo was another story.

"Tina told me you were planning to leave," she said.

Cole's wife had a lot to answer for. Keeping his expression neutral, he said, "Yes, ma'am, I am."

"Is Shay aware of this?"

"Yes."

"Are *you* aware you'll be breaking her heart?"

...you have to know I care about you.

What he had seen from Shay was a far cry from a broken heart. But now, he did see something else she had told him, in action right here. Her grandma was sticking up for her just the way she said Mo did, the way his father had never done for him.

Suddenly, he wished Cole hadn't left. His buddy could talk his way through a conversation like this one, while he'd never been good at discussing his feelings. He rested his elbows on his knees and linked his fingers together in front of him. "I'm not—" He stopped, cleared his throat, tried again. "I don't know what Shay told you."

"She hasn't told me anything, Tyler. She doesn't have to. I raised the lass, almost on my own."

The way Shay would raise their babies. He comforted himself with the thought she did have her grandma to help her.

"She's still in talking with Jed," Mo went on. "Once I see her, I'll only need to look at her to know how she feels. Just as I'm looking at you now and know how you're feeling. You're not happy."

He shrugged. "I've got a long drive ahead of me. I'll be happy when I put it behind me."

And you, at a distance.

That again. He had to stop replaying everything Shay had said. He had to forget Cole's unwanted advice and Mo's gentle insistence that she knew him better than he knew himself.

"Shay and I came to a mutual understanding," he assured her.

"Did you, now? Well, then, I suppose you'll both have to live with that."

What kind of life?

Now those were Cole's words, not Shay's. And not his. Trying to block out the noise in his head, he gripped his linked fingers so hard his knuckles cracked.

"Will you be seeing the babies before you leave?" Mo asked.

He swallowed hard. "No. I think it would be best if I don't."

"Well, perhaps you're right. Better to leave things as they are." She reached over to pat his arm. "This will be hard enough on you *and* them once you all realize the bond between you is broken."

TYLER WAS ALMOST done packing when a third knock came to the door. This one sounded less tentative than Mo's but not nearly as thunderous as Cole's. Again, his heart jumped to his throat.

Third time lucky?

He pushed the crazy thought aside and went to the door. His conclusion jumping aside, he had the distinct feeling he wouldn't find the woman he…the woman he could have found outside in the hallway.

Jed Garland stood with his thumbs in his belt loops and a smile on his face.

And now Tyler's heart sank. He let the man into the room, then took a quick look through the doorway. At this rate, he expected to find a line of Garland family members waiting their turn to enter. The hall was deserted. He closed the door and turned to Jed. "I don't think you're going to have to tell me why you're here. Let me guess. You talked to Tina."

"That I did."

"I thought Cole's wife was the quietest of your granddaughters."

Jed chuckled and went to the same seat Mo and Cole had taken.

This conversation wouldn't be as quick as the other two that had been held in the room this afternoon. He shoved his hands into his back pockets and sat on the end of the bed.

"So, you're on the run," Jed said.

Tyler eyed him suspiciously, wondering if the man had just made a judgment call about his decision. Jed rested his hands on the padded arms of the chair and sent him a level gaze. Tyler returned it. "You're here to try and convince me to stay."

"Nope. Haven't got an idea in the world about doing that."

At the older man's denial, he blinked in surprise. Shay's grandma and his own best friend both had made attempts. Maybe Jed wasn't the matchmaker he was cracked up to be. Or more likely, the man had meant what he said the day they had talked about Shay. "I'm glad you're not in any danger of destroying your winning streak."

Jed smiled. "So you remembered that? Yes, I'm

grateful for holding on to my record, too. And I'm just as glad not to ruin the reputation I've built."

So much for his earlier suspicions that Jed had been pulling strings to get him and Shay together.

"Some people are made to be matched," Jed continued, "and some aren't, and fortunately, I've got a sixth sense about which is which."

Why did that statement bother him? It wasn't like he had expected Jed to work harder. Or in his case, to work miracles. "Yeah. Well. Your sixth sense must have earned some overtime in the past week or so."

"It did. I guess you and Shay did some extra work these last few days, too. Taking care of one baby is a chore. Three must have really worn you down."

"It wasn't hard at all."

"No? Routine work, then—all those bottles and diapers and such."

"It wasn't routine, either. You'd think with the babies being triplets, they'd all behave the same. But they don't. They react to things in their own way. They don't look exactly alike, either."

"I don't know how you can figure that at their young age, except when it comes to telling Bree from her brothers, of course. I'd imagine those two boys get you all mixed up."

No, their *mother* got him all mixed up. "They're easy to tell apart. Timothy and Jamie look a lot alike, but they're not identical. Jamie's got more hair. Timothy's bigger and more active, although Jamie's catching up in both those departments. Bree—" He thought of her and smiled. "Bree's just a little sweetheart."

"That she is. It'll be amazing to watch how much they'll all change, even from one week to the next."

"Yeah." He wouldn't see that and didn't want to think about what he would miss. He tapped the duffel bag on the bed beside him. Shrugging, he said, "All of the kids look more like real little people every day. I've already seen lots of differences with each of them."

He would have the time he'd spent with the kids to help him remember them after he was gone. The time, and the photos from the local newspaper.

The article had been the talk of the Hitching Post's dining room this morning. As soon as breakfast was done, he had driven into town to get his own copy of the paper. The photos didn't show all the differences he'd learned about the babies, but he *had* learned them, and no one could take those memories away.

"Speaking of differences…"

Tyler looked up from his duffel bag to find Jed eyeing him.

"I gather you and Shay didn't have any luck patching up your differences."

"No." He tried not to frown.

"Just as well that you're leaving, then."

It's just as well, then. If you're not prepared to stay for the long haul, you might as well leave town.

Now, he did frown. He had expected that statement from Shay but hadn't seen the same reaction coming from Jed. The man really must value his reputation. "Yeah. Just as well. But I told you when we talked that I would do the right thing by Shay, and I am."

"That's good to hear."

"I'll be sending her money regularly."

"I'm sure it'll come in handy."

Handy? "She'll need the support. For the kids. For food and clothes and diapers and stuff."

"Well, yes. But I've arranged for her to take on more hours here at the hotel."

"So soon? She just delivered three babies. And they need her at home."

"Yes. But she wants the work."

"I can send her enough cash so that she won't have to add on hours yet."

Jed spread his hands palm up. "That's between the two of you. She'll do all right, though."

She won't need you. That's what Jed meant. He could hear it in the man's words and read it in his so-what gesture.

"Of course, money will get tighter as the triplets get bigger." Jed chuckled ruefully and shook his head. "I remember how it was with my three boys—just one thing after another. They'll constantly outgrow their clothes, quicker than Shay can turn around. And unlike my boys, she'll have three kids the same age. Not much chance of hand-me-downs in that family."

Was it getting hotter in here? He wiped his brow and stared at Jed. "I'll send her more money as the kids get older."

Jed nodded. "I reckon that might not be a bad idea. There will be doctor and dentist bills, a chance of braces and glasses, too. And then will come the day they all want cars and college."

Tyler exhaled heavily. Maybe he'd been wrong about the man. The way Jed was piling all that on, it seemed he was trying to scare him *away* from shouldering his responsibility. "You're right about all those things. But the babies aren't even a week old yet." He had said that to Shay, too. How could so little time have passed when he felt as though he'd gotten to know them all so well? "Aren't you jumping the gun, thinking about those things at this stage of the game?"

"That's just the thing. Raising kids isn't a game. Of course, there are lots of fun moments and rewards along the way, if we take the time to enjoy them."

Yeah, for the folks around *to enjoy them.*

"But that time is going to fly." Jed shook his head. "No, when all is said and done, caring for a family is a serious business. And it should only be done by folks who plan to take it seriously."

"I *will* take it seriously." He'd be responsible for his actions, would send Shay money for the kids. He would do the right thing to prove himself to Jed. To his parents. To himself.

...at a distance.

Chapter Seventeen

Shay set a plate of chocolate-chip cookies on the kitchen table and took her seat across from Layne. "Homemade, from Mrs. Browley." Mrs. Browley was one of Grandma's best friends and a regular at both SugarPie's and the Big Dipper.

"Oh, yum." Layne reached for a cookie. "I love these. And they're Jason's favorites."

"You'll have to take some home to him. We've got more food and desserts here than we can eat, thanks to our volunteers." Not one of them had dropped off a tray of baked ziti, though. The thought of Tyler's specialty made her mouth water. The thought of Tyler's mouth on hers made her press her lips together to keep them from trembling. She forced her gaze to Layne. "I'm glad you found some time to stop by."

"Going a little stir-crazy?"

And now Shay forced a laugh and reached for a cookie. "You don't know the half of it. Not that I mind being home alone with the babies," she added quickly.

"Of course not. But are you still alone?"

"Well, I shouldn't have put it that way. For the past few days, all our volunteers have shown up on schedule. This afternoon's helper left just a little while ago.

With Grandma off to her knitting circle, I really am happy for your visit."

She loved her friends and felt grateful for their volunteer time, too, but their attentions to her babies weren't the same as Tyler's. He had been out of their lives for three days now, and she knew the triplets missed him... because she missed him, too.

With a sigh, she pushed around the cookie she had dropped onto her plate.

"Have you heard from him?" Layne asked quietly.

She shook her head.

"You don't think getting in touch is worth a try?"

"You didn't hear him, Layne. He doesn't want to be around, even now that we have the babies." She winced, realizing what she had just unwittingly said. Layne's sad half smile said she had picked up on it, too.

She had to face the truth. Tyler hadn't wanted to stay around even before she had gotten pregnant.

"I don't have a way to get in touch with him, anyhow. We texted a few times when he was here for the wedding last summer, and then I... When I didn't hear from him, I deleted his texts and his number from my phone."

She had been upset then. She'd been more upset— and hurt—three days ago at the Hitching Post, the last time she had seen him.

"You could talk to Cole," Layne said. "For that matter, *I* could talk to Cole."

"No, thanks. Your brother is friends with Tyler. I don't want you—or me—to use him as a go-between."

"All he would be doing is passing along Tyler's phone number."

"No," she snapped. "If Tyler wants to talk to me, let him get in touch." With another sigh, she sank back in her chair. "I'm sorry, Layne, I don't know what's the matter with me."

"Don't apologize. I've been there, too, and not so long ago. And you know exactly what I'm talking about."

She nodded. "Yes, I do know." Layne definitely had suffered the symptoms of a broken heart, too.

"Then do you really need me to spell out your problem for you?"

"No. But you don't know the worst of it. I'm almost too embarrassed to tell you. We were so awful with each other that day." Poking at her cookie, she thought of the verbal jabs she and Tyler had thrown. She pushed the plate aside and stared at Layne. "I was so upset with myself for falling for a cowboy and so angry with him for leaving me last summer. For not wanting to stay now. But *he* was angry on behalf of the babies. He argued with me about them. He *fought* for them. Why would he have done that, why would he have tried so hard, if he didn't already care about them?"

"I think he does. But he's a mixed-up male who doesn't recognize his own feelings and probably wouldn't talk about them even if he did."

"He tried, I think. He started to talk to me, but I cut him off."

"Did he do the same to you?"

"Yes."

"Then you're even. Seriously. Don't try taking all the blame for what happened. You were both in the argument together."

That made sense, and yet it didn't fit—because Layne hadn't been there and didn't know the whole truth.

Tyler *did* care about the babies. He didn't love her, but

he loved his children. And she had been so unyielding, had pushed him so hard, he would never come back.

TYLER CROSSED THE barn to dump the bucket of water he'd been using to clean his tack.

Not knowing where else he wanted to go when he had left Cowboy Creek, he had returned to the ranch where he'd been working when he left Texas. With extra hands always needed for the spring roundup, the manager jumped on the chance to take him on again. He had hoped the return would let him settle for a while.

For more than a week, he had stayed almost too busy to think. Almost. He had acquired a steady job, a stall for Freedom, a place to rest his head at night. And still he had the sense of being more aimless than ever.

As he rinsed the sponge and set it on the shelf beside the utility sink, he thought about scrubbing pots in Shay and Mo's kitchen.

He had told Mo he would be happy when he had put his long drive home behind him. He hadn't lied, just hadn't realized the strategy wouldn't work.

Such a short time ago, it seemed wanderlust had sent him on the run, on the road to New Mexico. Maybe it wasn't wanderlust, after all. Maybe he *had* been running from something when he'd left Texas. But the visit to Cowboy Creek hadn't given him answers. In fact, it had only raised too many questions about worries he hadn't known existed for him until he had arrived.

And still, back in Texas again, he continued to feel unsettled.

"Hey, Buckham," one of the cowboys called across the barn. "We're heading to Roy's tonight for some wine, women and song."

"Forget the song," another of the hands called. "I'm just in it for the wine and women."

Somebody else snickered.

"Wanna join us?" the first man asked.

"I'll pass on this one." More proof things weren't right with him. Normally he'd have been the first one out the door headed to Roy's.

"Man, I don't know what happened on your trip to New Mexico. If I ever head that way, remind me not to drink the water."

More snickers.

That first afternoon in Cowboy Creek, he had stood in the ballroom at the Hitching Post with a glass of iced tea in his hand. He had looked at Shay and Tina, both pregnant, and jokingly asked himself if there was something in the water around there. If only he'd known then what he knew now.

Heck, if he'd known then what he'd known just a day or two later...

Most likely, even if he had heard sooner about Shay and the babies, nothing would have changed. He would have done the same things. He would have tried to do the *right* thing...and had it come out all wrong.

"I heard the boys talking about you the other night," one of the newer hands said to him. "They're all glad you're back, since you're the pasta expert on this spread."

Tyler forced a laugh. "Not an expert. I've only got one specialty. Baked ziti." Mo had loved it. Despite Shay's grudging nod, he was sure she had liked it, too. The woman wouldn't give an inch sometimes, even when it was in her own best interest.

"Yeah, that's what I'm talking about," the cowhand

said. "That ziti. If you're hanging around the bunkhouse tonight, maybe you ought to whip up a tray or two. Isn't it your turn to cook supper tomorrow?"

"Yeah. Sounds good. I'll run into town after I shower."

THE IDEA SOUNDED even better on his walk to the bunkhouse. Cooking would keep him busy. He had nothing else to do.

He thought of what had happened that afternoon he'd made the ziti at Shay's. She had come downstairs to the kitchen, where tea and toast had led to a kiss.

Frowning, he pushed the memory away.

At his bunk, he stripped off his shirt and went to his locker to gather what he needed for a shower. His gaze fell on the envelope on the top shelf. His hands stilled.

For a long moment, he looked at the envelope and fought the urge to take it down. A losing battle, as he had known it would be. He hadn't won the conflict once yet. Why should this time be different?

He sank onto the edge of his bunk and balanced the envelope on his knee. Two choices. Put it back and pretend it didn't exist. Or open it and wallow in self-pity.

He opened the flap. With two fingers, he pulled out the folded newspaper. He spread the paper wide and laid it across both knees.

"Hey, is that you?"

Tyler jumped. He hadn't heard the younger cowhand come into the bunkhouse. The man stood only a foot away. *Dang.* It was too late for him to hide the paper that had riveted his attention. "Yeah. That's me."

"Who all is that with you?"

He looked down again. "Family," he said.

From the front page of Cowboy Creek's local newspaper, Shay looked up at him. She sat in her wheelchair outside the hospital, cuddling Timothy and Jamie to her, the blue- and green-wrapped bundles looking so small in her arms. He stood behind the trio, holding Bree against him. The baby of all his babies looked—and was—even smaller than her brothers.

"Is that your sister?" the cowhand asked. "No wonder you had to take some time off, if she needed help. Families have to stick together, right?"

"Right." He didn't bother to correct the man's assumption. He didn't flinch as he agreed to something he hadn't done.

"Looks like she's got her hands full. And so do you."

"Yeah, we do."

The cowhand grabbed something from his locker and left the room.

Just as he'd done every night in this bunkhouse since his return, Tyler stared down at Shay's image. The photographer had caught her with her eyes crinkling at the corners and her smile wide as she laughed. She looked beautiful, happy, content. She looked like she was meant to be a mom.

He slid the newspaper back into the envelope and returned the envelope to his locker. He would rather have the photo out where he could see it, but it wasn't like he could frame it to hang on the wall or display on the shelf at the end of his bunk.

He'd gotten off easy with the new cowhand's faulty assumption. Some of the boys he'd worked with for a while here wouldn't have let the conversation go at that.

And what could he tell them? It was a picture of the woman and the kids he'd left behind?

Already, he missed the sight of the photo. He missed the babies. He missed their mom.

That restless feeling hit again.

He was back home, earning a living, still trying to do the right thing, but going at it all wrong. He had too many questions. And he wouldn't find his answers here.

AFTER MAKING SURE the baby monitor was working, Shay turned off the overhead light. She clicked the switch on the small lamp on the dresser. In the dimmed light, she stood and watched her babies sleeping.

Tyler had been gone just over a week. In that time, the triplets had grown and changed so much—in her eyes, at least. She noted each new fraction of an inch of fingernail, every additional ounce the babies drank at feeding time, all the extra minutes they now slept between feedings at night.

While she was grateful to have them sleeping more soundly, the minutes added up to more time alone for her. She spent too much of that time in her bedroom thinking of Tyler.

Sighing, she went downstairs.

Grandma sat in her rocker in the living room, working her knitting needles in her hands. "Are they all asleep now?"

"Yes." Shay took a seat on the couch and poured herself a cup of tea from the carafe on the table. The *Mom*s on her mug made her smile. The memory of Tyler coming into her hospital room with the mug and the stuffed animals was bittersweet.

"Good to see you looking happy, lass. What's on your mind?"

"I was just thinking about the days when the babies

won't be babies anymore. When they'll be toddlers running around the house and calling out 'Mommy' and 'Grandma.'"

"Let's not rush things, shall we? We have so many precious stages to experience before that happens."

"Oh, I'm not rushing anything." The slower time passed, the less Tyler would miss.

What would Grandma have said if she had shared the rest of her thoughts over this past week? She had envisioned the babies crawling, toddling, walking, going off to nursery school, to kindergarten and then to Cowboy Creek Elementary. Whether she rushed her thoughts or not, the triplets would grow so quickly. Soon, they would realize they were growing up without a daddy.

"You've stopped smiling," Grandma said. "You're not still with the babies. Now what's in your thoughts?"

She cradled the mug in her hands. "Nothing much."

"I taught you better than to give me a flip answer, Shay," Grandma said mildly. Shay flushed. "Should I have said *who's* in your thoughts?"

She shot a glance across the space, but Grandma's gaze focused on her knitting. There it was. The dead giveaway, the studied innocence that told her the question was anything but harmless. "And I know you better than that, Grandma. You could knit in your sleep."

Grandma laughed. "I think I have, at times." She set her project on the coffee table. "All right, let's stop talking circles around one another and go right to the point. You haven't been yourself this past week."

Shay opened her mouth, but Grandma held up a hand.

"Now, don't be citing chapter and verse to me about being a new mother, adjusting to new responsibilities, and losing out on sleep. Those are all true and valid points, but we both know they're not what's causing your distress. It's Tyler, isn't it?"

She wanted to deny it but couldn't. Silently, she nodded.

"I imagine you wanted Tyler to spend more time here."

She tried to bite her tongue to keep from responding but couldn't manage that, either. "No. I want him to *be* here. To *stay* here. For the babies' sakes."

"I'm sure you do. But you can't convince a person who doesn't want to change his mind."

"I know." Shay repeated what she had said to Layne. "He doesn't want to be around."

"Then you have to let him go."

"I did. I told him to leave, and he went."

"You're doing the right thing, love," Grandma said gently, "putting your babies first. But putting your feelings into words with Tyler is not what I meant. You have to let him go from your heart."

Chapter Eighteen

Last night, Tyler had cooked the requested trays of baked ziti. Tonight, he had left the cowhands at the ranch to enjoy it without him while he made the trek into Houston. He was forced to park his truck several blocks away from the towering building he planned to enter.

The streets were congested with cars and people. The air felt thick and heavy, weighing him down, and even the late-afternoon sunlight didn't seem as bright as it did out on the ranch.

The building's lobby doors automatically swished closed behind him, cutting him off from civilization. As the elevator slammed shut, it seemed to swallow him up. Nothing had changed. He had hated everything about this place when he lived here and didn't like it any better now.

Once off the elevator, he strode down the hall to a shiny-clean white door with a gleaming brass bell plate. He rang the bell and waited. Part of him hoped no one was home.

He didn't belong here. He never had. The road had taken him to a life spent doing what he did best. Rodeo, wrangling, and everything else a cowboy did. Everything Shay didn't like.

After a few minutes, the door swung open.

The look of surprise on his mother's face didn't fool him. She would have checked the security peephole in the door. And she must have recognized him. After all, he'd just been there a few months ago for Christmas.

"Mom."

"Tyler." She wore one of the long, floaty dresses she always changed into for supper—*dinner*—every evening. Her hair looked perfect, her makeup immaculate. She tilted her head to accept the kiss he left somewhere in the air near her cheek. Stepping back, she swung the door wide. "Do come in. Your father's not here. He should be home shortly. Can I get you something to drink?"

He blinked. An excited smile or a spontaneous hug would have been too much to expect. Still, he had thought his appearance would warrant more than the standard cocktail-party greeting. "No, I'm good." He didn't care for cocktails, anyway. And they wouldn't have beer in the house.

"You'll excuse me if I make myself one."

It wasn't a question, but he nodded. She headed in the direction of the kitchen. He looked around him, taking in the room he had been happy to escape years ago. Glass and chrome, lacquer and acrylic. The furnishings and decorations were the same throughout the condo, even in his bedroom.

As a kid, he couldn't breathe with so much fake glare and glitter around him. One weekend, he had pasted nature and rodeo posters all over his bedroom, including the mirrored doors of the wall-to-wall closet. When his mother discovered it and told his father what he had done, he'd been grounded for a month. He had spent every evening after supper alone in his room with a bucket of water and a paint scraper. The fee the condo management charged to refurbish the room had come from his allowance. His father had wanted him to learn a lesson.

He *had* learned one—that a condo in Houston wasn't where he wanted to be. As soon as he had finished high school, he had moved out, found a job wrangling and spent weekends and whatever free time he could get following the rodeo.

His mother returned from the kitchen, her slippers tapping on the tile floor. She carried a tray with a bucket filled with ice and a bottle. Alongside the bucket sat two crystal tumblers. Ice tinkled as she set the tray down on the glass-topped coffee table. They took seats on opposite sides of the table, and she poured herself a drink.

"It's been a while since we've seen you," she said, skipping over the part about their uncomfortable holiday reunion. He and his father had never gotten along well, and he had always hated his parents' fake merriment of the season, too. They couldn't even get a real tree. "What have you been up to?"

He swallowed a laugh. Where would he start? Might as well go straight to the highlights. "I've got some news for you and Dad. I'm… I'm a daddy myself now."

She blinked. He had inherited the same shade of blue eyes. "What? Why…? Why didn't you tell us this when you were here for Christmas?"

"I didn't know then."

The condo door opened. Tyler John Buckham Sr.—called John his whole life—stepped into the living room.

His eyebrows went up at the sight of his son sitting on the couch. "Tyler."

Tyler rose and they shook hands. He had gotten his dark hair from his father and would someday get the silver streaks, too. Probably sooner than he anticipated, considering what had happened lately.

"We weren't expecting you."

"Sorry. Should I have called in advance?"

His father's eyes narrowed. He leaned down to pick up the extra tumbler from the tray. Tyler took his seat again.

As his mother poured a drink, she said, "John, Tyler has news for us. He's become a father."

Still standing and now blank faced, Tyler's dad looked at him. "Is that so? Why is this the first we've heard of it?"

"As I told Mom, I didn't know it myself. I just found out a few weeks ago." He took the folded-up newspaper from his back pocket and handed it across the table.

His mother took it and looked down at the front-page photo. She let out a gasp. "Tyler! Are these *all* yours?"

"All?" His father took the newspaper from her and glanced at it, then at Tyler again. "*Three* children? So that's why you're here."

For a moment, Tyler was taken aback. He should have expected the reaction. Playing daddy had made him forget what his own father was like. Had also made him forget why he wasn't cut out to be a dad himself. "Yes. That's partly why I'm here. I wanted you and Mom to know."

"And the other part? You want help taking care of these kids, I suppose."

I don't want your charity. Shay had told him that. Suddenly, he knew how she felt.

"Why else would you be here?" his father went on. "You can't possibly raise three kids on what you make."

"I'll manage."

"Does your wife work?"

"We're not married. We're not together."

His father stared at him. "Then what was this, a one-night stand? And now you've got three children to support, all at once. What were you thinking, Tyler?"

"I wasn't expecting three kids, that's for sure."

"Watch that backtalk."

"Dad." He forced his jaw to unclench. "I couldn't have controlled how many babies came along."

"You could have controlled yourself. At the very least, you could have been responsible enough to use protection."

He had him there. He'd nailed it all. It *had* been a one-night stand, a good time that wasn't supposed to turn into anything else. Instead, it had led to more than Tyler could believe. "Protection doesn't always work. But no, I didn't use it. The point is, the babies are here now."

"And you're expecting us to help you out."

"No, I'm not. I told you, I wanted you and Mom to hear the news. I thought you would be happy to have grandkids, that you might want to see them." He rose from his seat and grabbed the newspaper from his father's hand. "I should have known better. You're not even happy to have a son, let alone grandkids."

"Tyler—"

"Forget it. We all know I'll never be good enough to measure up to your standards. I've just figured out my kids never will, either—because you won't give them a chance. But they won't ever know that. I'll make sure to keep them away from here."

He was careful not to slam the condo door as he left. He was more careful not to run.

Hadn't he done that enough times already? He had taken off from his parents' home at seventeen, run from Texas just a couple of weeks ago. Worst of all, he had left Shay again, just as he had soon after they had met. This time, she had told him to go. But he hadn't argued.

The elevator doors slammed shut. He stared at his reflection in the stainless-steel doors. He didn't like what he saw, and he liked even less the way he felt inside.

This visit home proved what he had known all his life. He couldn't be the son his parents wanted him to be.

He wasn't the man Shay wanted for herself or their kids.

Out on the street again, the heavy air made it hard for him to take a deep breath. Or maybe the struggle came from the tightness like a band across his chest.

He couldn't exist the way he had been living, couldn't keep feeling so aimless and unsettled, couldn't keep running. It was time to figure out who he was and what *he* wanted.

SHAY SAT ON the bed in the hotel suite she and Jed's granddaughters used to prepare for weddings held at the Hitching Post. She leaned back against the headboard and shifted a couple of the sample books she had spread out around her.

At the sound of heavy footsteps in the hallway, she looked up expectantly. It sounded like Jed. It was her first day back to work since he had given her extra hours and, knowing him, he wanted to make sure she wasn't overdoing it.

It was also three weeks since Tyler had left…but she didn't want to think about that.

Sure enough, the minute Jed walked into the room, he gave her his usual smile and said, "How are you doing, girl?"

She spread her arms wide, her palms up, gesturing at the suite. "Living a life of ease, thanks to you, boss."

He chuckled as he took the chair at the desk adjacent to the bed. "That's what I like to hear. And the babies?"

"They're wonderful. They're nearly a month old already, and they just had another checkup yesterday. Dr. Grayden says they're doing fine. They've grown so much. They've gotten so strong." She thought of Tyler's excitement over Jamie's grip…and pushed the vision aside. "Grandma and I have been exercising the babies. She says moving their legs—as if they were riding a bicycle—will help strengthen the triplets' muscles for when they're ready to crawl and then to walk."

"You're going to have your hands full when that day comes." He smiled. "I'm planning to stop by to see them again soon."

"I wish you would."

He nodded. "In the meantime, don't you wear yourself out. Mo and Paz both would have my hide if they thought I was running you into the ground."

"No chance of that. This is easy work compared to mommying three infants."

"And I'm sure you would much rather be home doing that than working here."

She would, but she could never say that to Jed. His generosity was going to help her take care of those infants. Instead she laughed. "It's a moot point, since I didn't have a chance of staying home, anyway. You should have seen Grandma shooing me out the door. And our volunteer for the day hadn't even arrived yet."

"Mo wanted some time with her great-grandbabies, I'll bet."

"Yes, I think you're correct—Grandma did want the babies to herself."

"That's only right. Grandparents need that alone time."

So did daddies.

"I didn't like it at all," he went on, "when my three boys left Cowboy Creek, especially when two of them got married and then Jane and Andi came along. I was glad whenever they came to visit."

"I'm sure you were. It must have been so nice for you to have Tina grow up right here."

"It was. I learned more about her quicker than I did with the other girls. But that doesn't mean I didn't get to learn about them, too. Every time they arrived, though, it came as a shock to see how much they had changed."

If Tyler never visited, he wouldn't face those shocks. He wouldn't see any of the changes or the stages their babies went through. "They do grow fast," she murmured.

"They do," he agreed. "And they're all so different, just like your three little ones. But of course I love all my girls, just the way you love your babies." He smiled. "Tina always was the one with her nose in a book, yet she also had a good head for numbers. Jane was the artist in the family, always drawing or painting—sometimes on the other girls' books."

They both laughed.

"I'll probably have to face some of that, too," she said.

"I reckon you will. Most likely, you'll also have one

of the three who's a peacemaker, like Andi. Tina never was one to get riled, except those times Jane drew all over her books. Andi could always get in between the other two girls and calm them down."

"That will be Bree, I'm sure. She's more relaxed about everything. Tyler says—" She stopped short.

As if he hadn't noticed, Jed spoke again. "That's the thing about babies. Triplets or not, they can all pretty much seem alike when they're so tiny. It's only after they grow a bit that you get to see they have their own ways. And of course, the older they get, the more evident that becomes. With Tina and Jane and Andi, I never could have predicted exactly how they would turn out or what they would eventually do with their lives."

"That's not completely true." She grinned. "You more than predicted who they would marry."

He laughed. "So I did. Well, after all, those couples needed a few nudges along the way. But I'd never have gotten involved if I didn't think the matches were meant to be."

She froze in the process of shifting one of the sample books aside.

Was that why Jed hadn't helped her? Did he believe she and Tyler wouldn't make a good pair?

"The point is," he continued, "you have to respect those differences. You have to stand back and let your grandkids—and your kids—manage on their own."

It seemed almost as if Jed had overheard her argument with Tyler.

I think you're controlling their futures—

When Tyler had begun to speak, she had cut him off. Now she would never know what else he might have added. She would never know if he might have been right.

She looked at Jed. "You have to help guide your kids as they grow up, though."

"Of course you do. But, within reason, you've also got to let them make their own choices and their own mistakes. Aside from that, all you can do is love them and be there when they need you."

Her babies would need a daddy, too, but they wouldn't have one. They would have her to blame for that. "I'll always be here for my kids."

"I have no doubts about that." He smiled at her, his clear blue eyes holding her gaze.

"And I think I've got your message, boss," she said softly. "I should have expected you to try a little reverse psychology. You did everything you could to bring us together, didn't you? Including leaving Tyler on his own the night of the wedding?"

He chuckled but said nothing else.

Jed was helping, after all. He was teaching her about love and acceptance…and learning from mistakes.

Suddenly, she realized Grandma had used the same tactics on her.

You have to let him go from your heart.

She couldn't let Tyler go. He was in her heart and always would be.

She stared back at Jed. "You and Grandma know exactly how I feel about Tyler, don't you?"

"I think we do."

She sighed. "I've messed things up, Jed. Tyler left because I told him to go."

He reached across the bed to pat her hand. "Nobody can fault you for that, girl. No matter how you feel, you need to do what's right for the babies. And you *are* doing the right thing by putting them first."

Her eyes misted. She blinked the moisture away.

Grandma had said the same thing in just those words. She and Jed *were* trying to help, by forcing her to see her mistakes for herself.

Her worst mistake of all had come from not trusting Tyler.

Chapter Nineteen

The minute she finished up her work, Shay rushed out to her car. This was the first day she had driven it since Tyler had picked her and the triplets up at the hospital. The outside was still shiny and clean. The inside still smelled faintly of his aftershave. She gripped the wheel and sped away from the Hitching Post.

This was also the first time she had been separated from the babies since the day they were born. The few hours apart from them had seemed endless.

The weeks Tyler had been gone felt like an eternity.

At the house, all three triplets were fast asleep in their cribs.

She could envision Tyler reaching down to lift Timothy or Jamie or Bree, always moving so carefully as he carried one of them across the room. She could see him with a bundle in the crook of his arm as he bottle-fed a baby. She recalled him changing a pair of pajamas and muttering about the tiny fastenings.

He'd resisted learning to change a diaper, though. Her laugh at that thought ended on a small sob. Now he would never learn.

By the time the babies began to wake and look for

a feeding, she was more than ready to cuddle each one to her.

Grandma walked into the bedroom just as Shay kissed Bree and tucked her back into the crib. "Giving that one a little extra loving, are you?"

Yes. The extra loving Bree was missing from her daddy. She forced a smile. "You can never give too much."

"That's true enough."

Tyler had been proud of Timothy for being the strong big brother and had encouraged Jamie, the smaller of the two boys, to stretch and grow. But whether he had realized it or not, he had developed a special bond with his daughter.

Gonna be a heartbreaker someday.

Bree had become Daddy's little girl.

"And what's going on with you, love?" Grandma crooned to Timothy. She gestured to the crib. "Just see what our big boy has done, Shay."

Shay moved closer. Timothy had kicked off the light blanket she had draped over him. "I think that exercise we've been giving him is paying off." She lifted him, holding him upright with his feet just above the mattress. He flexed his legs, kicking so energetically his tiny feet pushed the covers aside.

"I do believe we've just seen him reach a milestone," Grandma said softly.

"I think you're right." Shay's voice sounded shaky. Her laugh cracked in the middle. Her eyes flooded with tears she fought to blink away. "Here, Grandma. Maybe you'll have better luck tucking him in than I did. I'll be right back."

Brushing at her eyes, she left the room.

The thought of all the milestones, of all the progress the babies would make without their daddy to see them, had broken her.

She went down the hall to her bedroom. Her cell phone sat on the corner of the dresser. She grabbed it and touched the screen to bring up the last number she had called.

The phone on the other end rang and rang, finally switching to voice messaging. Swallowing a sigh of impatience, she waited for the recorded message to end.

At the beep, she took a deep breath, brushed away her tears again and said, "Layne, when you get this, please call me. I need to talk."

THE SUN WAS just setting when Tyler pulled up and parked at the curb in front of the small two-story house. Lights shone through the front window curtains, and music floated through the open window. Flowers in boxes attached to the porch railing bobbed in the breeze, reminding him of the balloons tied to the mug he had bought for Shay. The air smelled of those flowers and fresh earth, and above that of garlic and tomatoes, probably from supper bubbling on the stove.

It was all so different from the big city and his parents' place. Here, he could breathe.

When he rang the bell, the sound of the radio lowered.

"I'll get it, Grandma," Shay called from inside the house. "It's probably Jed."

A minute later, the door swung open. She stood there with her hand gripping the door the way she had the day he'd come home…come back from his shopping trip. The day he had kissed her. Suddenly, he couldn't breathe at all.

Her eyes were huge and glowing. "You...you're here."

He coughed out a breath, looked down at himself, then up again. Not smiling, he said, "Yeah. So I am. Can we talk?"

She frowned, and his heart thudded against his breastbone. Looking puzzled, she stepped onto the porch.

"Wait," he said. "Could we talk upstairs?"

"In the babies' room?"

He nodded. "I want to see the kids."

She stared past him to the flowers blowing in the breeze, yet her gaze seemed unfocused. "They'll want to see you."

They, not *we*.

But she turned and went back inside. It was a start.

He followed her through the living room and up the stairs, his heart hammering harder than it should have after so little exertion.

On the landing, he reached out to put his hand on her shoulder to stop her from walking down the hall. Instantly, the warmth of her made him a little crazy, made him want to take her into his arms and kiss her until she agreed to everything he was going to ask her tonight.

Sanity made him drop his hand and step back. "Before we go in there, I have to tell you something. I want more than just this one visit, Shay. I want to see the babies whenever I can. I want to know I'm part of their lives." He braced himself, knowing that after the way he had left her—again—he would have to fight for his rights. Would have to face the risk of losing both the battle and something very precious in the process.

Stunned, he watched her nod.

"You *are* part of their lives. I'm not going to stand in the way of you seeing them."

It was more than he could have hoped for. More than he deserved.

In the babies' room, he went directly to the cribs. All three were awake, probably ready for yet another feeding. He lifted Bree from the crib and held her against him.

There's my little girl, he wanted to say, but didn't.

"She's…bigger," he managed.

"Yes." Shay's features softened in a small smile. "When you're only a month old, a few weeks make a huge difference."

"Are their checkups going okay?"

"They're great." And now he saw the full smile he had been waiting for.

He wanted to reach out and touch her cheek. Instead, he brushed Bree's head lightly with his fingertips. "She has curls."

"They all do, now that their hair has grown a bit."

Bree turned her head, nestling against him the way she had before he had left. His chest swelled with pride. "She remembers me." His voice shook.

"I was just getting their bottles." Shay's voice sounded wobbly, too. "Do you want to hold her while I go downstairs?"

"Yeah, I do." He wanted much more than that.

One step at a time.

Shay's question felt like a nod of acceptance. It gave him hope that coming back here had been the right thing to do.

He hadn't lied. He wanted to see the babies whenever he could. Being a part of their lives had become more important to him than he could have believed possible. But as much as that would mean to him, it wasn't enough.

He wanted his return to lead to something he might never be able to earn—a permanent place in Shay's life, too.

When she left the room, he carried the baby over to the rocking chair in the corner. "What am I gonna do, Bree?" he asked quietly. "I hurt your mom last summer. I hurt her a lot. And now I want to win her back." Bree stared up at him.

The nurse at the hospital had told him babies this age couldn't see very far. He held Bree up closer to his face. She kept her gaze fastened on him. "It's not going to be easy, I know that. First, I'm going to have to make amends…somehow. And then…your mom said I wasn't in this for the long haul. Maybe I didn't have an answer at the time, but I have one now. I'm with you and your brothers for life."

He watched her closely. "It'll take some doing to convince your mom I'm not just making empty promises. But when all is said and done, she'll believe me, don't you think?"

The baby squirmed in his arms. Her eyes crinkled shut. Her mouth pursed, then curved up at the corners. He didn't care what Cole said—his little girl had just smiled at him.

He kissed her forehead. "Thanks for the vote of confidence, Bree."

From downstairs, he heard the doorbell, followed by Shay's voice and another, deeper voice he recognized.

A minute later, he heard Jed's boots on the stairs.

The older man appeared in doorway. "Well, look

who's back." He crossed the room, his hand outstretched. Tyler shook hands with him. "Couldn't stay away, could you, boy?"

"No, I couldn't," he admitted.

"I can't say as I blame you, with three little ones like these. If they were mine, I'd come home, too."

"Home?"

Jed smiled. "They say that's where your heart is."

Tyler looked down at Bree, then over at the boys in their cribs, and finally at the woman who had just walked through the doorway.

Jed was right. He had come back to Cowboy Creek because this is where he'd found both his heart and his home.

SHAY WATCHED TYLER move restlessly around the babies' room. He looked like he wanted to run, the way he had not once but twice before.

Grandma had come upstairs to greet Jed. They all chatted for a few minutes, then the two of them had gone downstairs for a glass of sweet tea before supper. By that time, Shay had fed the babies. Tyler had thought Bree was ready to go first this time, and Shay had agreed. Timothy had followed, and Jamie had eaten last.

She tucked Jamie into the crib and returned to the rocking chair. "You'll stay for supper?" she asked Tyler.

He turned to her. "Yes, I will." He cleared his throat and shoved his hands into his back pockets. "In case you were wondering where I went when I left, I went back to Texas, to the ranch where I'd been working. But things weren't the same as when I'd been there before. *I* wasn't the same."

"Becoming a daddy must make you look at everything differently. I know becoming a mom has had that effect on me."

"That's part of it." He crossed the room to her and took a seat on the footstool she had put aside. The small lamp on the dresser made his hair a glossy black. The pearl snaps on his shirtfront winked at her, and his champion belt buckle shone in the light.

"The other part is," he went on, "I've been feeling restless for a long time without knowing why. The feeling kicked in last summer, when I came here for the wedding and spent time with all the Garlands. And with you. Once I left, the feeling got worse instead of better."

She held her breath.

He smiled. "I think being around the Hitching Post made me see what I was missing. A family. And being with you made me want something I'd never wanted before. A place to settle for good."

"Then…then why didn't you come back?" Her voice broke.

"I didn't know all this last summer. I didn't know it even a few weeks ago." He wouldn't meet her eyes. "It wasn't until I left this time that I figured out what was wrong." He rested his elbows on his knees and linked his fingers together in front of him. "While I was back in Texas, I took a trip to see my folks."

"How did that go?"

He stared down at his hands. "Badly. But nothing worse than I might've imagined. I told you my parents never had my back, that my father pushed me."

When he didn't continue, she said, "I remember. You said he tried to make a man out of you."

"Yeah. But it wasn't the kind of man I wanted to be. And I wasn't the son they wanted. My father's a corporate lawyer with a big salary and the clothes and cars and condo to go with it. My entire life, my parents attempted to talk me into following in his footsteps. I tried. I tried to accept their views and their idea of success. Finally, I got to the point where I couldn't do that anymore. Because they're not *my* views."

Now, he looked at her, his eyes shining in the lamplight. "Shay, I might have grown up in a city, but I'm a born cowboy. That's the life I want. But I don't want to live that life alone." He took her hand and brushed his thumb across her knuckles. "I gave up the job in Texas—again. Permanently, this time. I talked to the manager at the hardware store here in town. He said he might have an opening coming up. He also gave me the name of a couple of local distributors he works with, said they're always looking for folks to do outside sales." He squeezed her fingers. "I'll do anything I have to, to prove to you I'm ready to settle down. I want roots. I want a family—*our* family."

Her eyes flooded. She blinked but couldn't hold back tears. He wiped them away. "Oh, Tyler." Her exhalation sounded more like a sob. "You already *have* proven yourself—to me and to everyone else who has met you here. I told you, we can all see what a good man you are, just by the way you care about our babies." She squeezed his fingers. "You must have believed me, or you wouldn't have come back."

His eyebrows came together in a puzzled frown. "You told me?"

"Yes. In my message."

"What message?"

She blinked. "On your phone. I had Layne get your number from Cole, and I called you this morning."

"I haven't looked at my phone since I left my parents' house last night. I heard a call come in earlier today and figured it was my father, wanting to ram his point home about how irresponsible I'd been." Suddenly, he laughed. "You left me a message?" he said wonderingly.

She nodded. "I told you just what I said now—that we all know you're a good man. And," she added softly, "I asked you to come back so we could talk things out."

"I'm here now."

She nodded again.

"Does that mean you've forgiven me for leaving you—twice?"

"Yes." She laced her fingers through his. "And I hope you'll forgive me for how I treated you when you came back. I'm sorry, Tyler. I was so wrong to push you away just because of what you do—of who you *are*. And you were right. I *was* holding my own experience with my dad against you. When I kept comparing you to him, I never really gave you a chance." She sighed. "I'm as bad as your parents are, not accepting your choices."

"You didn't know about them."

"No, but I know about me and how overly sensitive I am about cowboys and the rodeo. I also know you were right about my controlling the babies' future. Or at least, that's what I seemed to be doing, only because I was too determined to justify my feelings and to win the argument." She blinked a few times, then stared at him again. "I wouldn't try to run my own children's— our children's—lives. I'm so sorry I tried to do that to you, too."

"Does that mean I won't have to give up wrangling?"

She laughed. "Yes, that's what it means. I believe in

you, Tyler. And if you ever listen to my phone message, you'll know that I love you."

He smiled. "I love you, too."

He cupped her face in his hands and brushed his mouth against hers, kissing her the way she loved to begin, soft and easy and sweet. But this time there was a hint of the spice she loved, too. It felt like a promise offered and accepted, a promise that wouldn't break.

She put her hands on his shoulders and tilted her head back to look up at him. "You know," she said with a smile, "I've decided I would be content to have our babies follow in your footsteps."

"Become cowboys, you mean?" When she nodded, he laughed. "Well, it's up to them, of course." She nodded again. "But if that's what any or all of them choose, it's fine with me. Because my footsteps won't ever take me far from home."

Epilogue

Two months later

In the banquet hall of the Hitching Post, Tyler stood looking around him. Everything had turned out perfectly, according to Shay, who had told him more than once she was over the moon with happiness.

He was just glad his new bride hadn't had to do any of the work to prepare for their wedding. In fact, she had given up her job at the hotel, for now anyway, to stay home with their babies.

If her former boss resented the fact, he wasn't letting on.

Jed looked darned good in his tuxedo and cummerbund.

Tyler smiled. The man had given Tina away to Cole at their ceremony last year...at the wedding where he had first met Shay. "You're making a habit of walking brides down the aisle."

"It's great advertising for his business," Shay said with a laugh.

"The Hitching Post can use the plug," Jed agreed.

"I meant the *matchmaking* business."

Now Jed and Tyler laughed.

As Jed walked away, Tyler looked across the dance floor to one of the tables at the front of the room. Shay had convinced him to extend a wedding invitation to his parents, and to his surprise, they had accepted. They sat at the table with Mo and Sugar. All four of them had their heads bent over the baby books Mo had brought to show off to everyone at the reception.

Pictures were nice, but he looked forward to seeing the kids upstairs later, where Pete's housekeeper was minding them for the evening.

"What do you think?" Shay asked.

She was looking in that direction, too.

"For the babies' sakes, I think I can make an effort to get along." The band struck up another slow song. He took her into his arms. "Speaking of getting, you're happy you got your June wedding?"

"Of course I am. It's something I've dreamed about my entire life. And so are you."

Her unconditional support was all he ever could have wanted, too. "That's little enough to give you, after everything you've given me. Love and a home and a family. And you've made today the best day of my life."

"I've done more than that."

He smiled down at her. Her eyes sparkled. "I'll say. You carried our kids for almost nine months and brought them into this world."

"And named them Timothy and Jamie and Bree."

"So you did."

"Timothy. Jamie. And Bree," she said with soft emphasis.

"Great names. Timothy. Ja—" He stopped short in the middle of the dance floor, hardly believing the mental leap he had just made. "Timothy. Jamie. Bree. Tyler

John Buckham," he said, his voice cracking. "You gave them my initials."

She nodded. "I decided on that the day the doctor told me I was carrying three babies."

"The day—?" His throat grew so tight, he couldn't speak. He waited a moment and tried again. "Even after I'd left all those months ago?"

"Even after. I wanted them to have a connection to you." She rested her cheek against his chest. He tilted his head down to hear her voice over the music. Her breath tickled his ear. "Even when I wanted to hate you, I loved you, Tyler. When the doctor told me the news, I was still upset about your leaving, about realizing I might never see you again and that the babies might never know you. But I also realized you were part of them and always would be." She raised her head to meet his eyes.

He saw her through a blur. He blinked, cleared his throat and smiled. "I love Timothy and Jamie and Bree."

"I know you do."

He held her closer. "I love you, Shay. I'll always be here for you and the kids."

She smiled. "I believe you, cowboy. And we all love you, too."

* * * * *

Look for the next book in
THE HITCHING POST HOTEL *series in May 2017 wherever Harlequin books and ebooks are sold!*

SPECIAL EXCERPT FROM

(H) HARLEQUIN®

𝒲estern Romance

*Ranch manager Easton Ross was always there for
Nora Carpenter, but she left Hope, Montana, and never
looked back. Now she's home with three adorable
newborns, and Easton is in trouble—he's falling for her
all over again.*

*Read on for a sneak preview of
THE TRIPLETS' COWBOY DADDY,
the latest book in Patricia Johns's series
HOPE, MONTANA.*

Nora Carpenter could have cared for one baby easily
enough. She could somehow have juggled two. But
three—she'd never imagined that accepting the role of
godmother to her half sister's babies would actually put
her in the position of raising those babies on her own. She
was still in shock.

Nora stood in her mother's brilliantly clean farmhouse
kitchen, more overwhelmed than she had ever felt in her
life. The three infants were still in their car seats, eyes
scrunched shut and mouths open in hiccuping wails. She
stood over them, her jeans already stained from spilled
formula and her tank top stretched from…she wasn't even
sure what. She unbuckled the first infant—Rosie—and
scooped her up. Rosie's cries subsided as she wriggled up
against Nora's neck, but anxiety still made Nora's heart
race as she fumbled with Riley's buckle. She'd come

back to Hope, Montana, that afternoon so that her mother could help her out, but even that was more complicated than anyone guessed. These babies weren't just orphans in need of care; they were three tiny reminders that Nora's father hadn't been the man they all believed him to be.

The babies' cries echoed through the house.

Rosie, Riley and Roberta had finished their bottles just before Nora's mother had left for a quick trip to the store for some baby supplies.

"I'll be fine!" Nora had said. Famous last words. The minute the door shut, the cries had begun, and no amount of cooing or rocking of car seats made a bit of difference.

There was a knock on the back door, and Nora shouted, "Come in!" as she scooped up Riley in her other arm and cuddled both babies close. Riley's cries stopped almost immediately, too, and that left Roberta—Bobbie, as Nora had nicknamed her—still crying in her car seat, hands balled up into tiny fists.

Nora had no idea who was at the door, and she didn't care. Whoever walked through that door was about to be put to work. Served them right for dropping by.

"Need a hand?" The voice behind her was deep—and familiar. Nora turned to see Easton Ross, the family's ranch manager, standing in the open door.

Don't miss THE TRIPLETS' COWBOY DADDY
by Patricia Johns, available April 2017 wherever
Harlequin® Western Romance
books and ebooks are sold.

www.Harlequin.com

Turn your love of reading into
rewards you'll love with
Harlequin My Rewards

**Join for FREE today at
www.HarlequinMyRewards.com**

Earn **FREE BOOKS** of your choice.

Experience **EXCLUSIVE OFFERS** and contests.

Enjoy **BOOK RECOMMENDATIONS**
selected just for you.

PLUS! Sign up now
and get **500** points
right away!

Earn
FREE
REWARDS
HarlequinMyRewards.com
Join
Today!

MYR16R